THE EERIE EGG

SIR PATRICK BIJOU

BOOK DESCRIPTION

Overweight, unloved, bullied, and an undesirable virgin are just some of the things that describe high schooler Jacob Grand... but not for long.

Jacob Grand can't seem to catch a break.

He's being bullied in school, his father blames him for his mother's death, and no girl would touch him with a ten-foot pole.

It goes without saying that Jacob now suffers from a slew of insecurities, anxieties, and numbness.

And with a father who abuses him constantly, Jacob's only solace is a log along a quiet creek in his hometown's scenic forest.

One day, as he basks in the solitude of his special place, Jacob is thrust into unfortunate circumstances again. This time though, something out of this world happens.

A kind voice seeped into the darkness of his mind. It showed empathy for his pain and gave him instructions on what to do next.

Understandably, Jacob couldn't determine if the voice was real or just a particular coping mechanism. But he listened anyway.

And so begins a series of strange and hyper-erotic dreams, those of which leave him with wildly carnal desires and appetites upon waking.

What he doesn't anticipate, however, is that this is just the beginning of the rest of his life. There are many things in store for Jacob... much, much more.

"The Eerie Egg" is a scintillating suspense thriller erotica of a young boy's journey toward manhood — with an extraterrestrial twist that will drive any reader's imagination wild with desire.

If you're looking for a thrilling read filled with sex, gore, and horny aliens, get ready to meet your next favourite book!

ABOUT THE AUTHOR

I HAVE SOMETHING TO TELL

His Excellency Sir Patrick Bijou lives and writes from the United Kingdom and is the author of several books on finance and fiction. He is known for his extraordinary skills in settling and negotiating peace settlements and international law and is a prodigious legal and political adviser. His diverse writing ability has been influenced by many experiences, making him the success he is today.

Sir Patrick has written many books and articles about the liberation of people, highlighting the issues of those whom the literary world of creative writing has not enlightened. His expedition into content writing has made him a remarkably inspired author and professional communicator.

He has written over 31 non-fictional and fictional books spanning different genres.

Finding his Books.

To find out more about Sir Patrick, visit his website.

www.sirpatrickbijou.com
www.bijouebook.com

The woods that made up Verdant Springs could be called eerie. A mix of tall old birches and pines that grew thicker the deeper on traveled off the paved paths that wove through it. Moss grew in great blankets across the ground broken by small game trails and paths.

The young boy who walked down a dirt path didn't find the deep wood eerie, but a refuge. Dried tears clung to the boy's cheek as he navigated the path as hastily as possible. The faraway laughter of other people tormented him as he sought a favorite sanctuary. In his mind, any laughter heard A small creek that carved its bed through the woods.

Jacob Grand walked down the path into his sullen self. A look that he wore just like the big baggy clothes and thick-rimmed glasses he sported. At five-foot-nine, Jacob's obese frame often meant comparisons to a whale. Grand he couldn't be called except maybe if his expanding waistline counted. To the jocks, it counted.

"Why?" Jacob said out loud.

Jacob asked the question a lot to himself. To the bullies who tortured him at school, peers who ignored him, to his father who either neglected or beat him. No answer ever came back that made it easier. Just more insults to flying fists.

He walked, his feet finding precarious perches as he did. Sore legs carried him through. Hurting, Jacob felt a feeling of elation as he cleared the last of the trees and saw the bend in the creek that he loved.

The bend that Jacob loved could only be seen from the opposite bank. Years ago, Jacob had built a makeshift bridge, which as he crossed currently, wobbled and bucked under his weight. There may have been a crack, but it fell on deaf ears.

In the small clearing that made up his favorite spot sat a single log. Next to that happened to be an old military box made out of metal and weather-sealed. A stake had been driven through the bottom to anchor it and a rusting lock kept the weather seal locked and in place. Inside the box, Jacob stored an assortment of writing materials and books. Today wouldn't be a day that he opened the box, instead, he would sulk on the log.

Many a day Jacob had sat on the log. Peace here in the creek always brought him out of the pains the world offered him. The lazy way water flowed over polished black rocks or how limbs of trees bathed their leaves in pleasant breezes left him with a serene feeling. A feeling washed over him quickly and he sat listening to the flow of water in the creek.

After a bit, Jacob's stomach growled in impatience. It always did that though. Growling and bothering him with its insatiable appetite, Jacob knew what it wanted down to not only a habit but taste. Taking his pack off and opening it, he pulled out a lunch box that was cold to touch. The opening revealed a carefully protected prize.

The roast beef sandwich sat in a plastic lock bag. Already Jacob could taste the sandwich. Laid with prime cut, lettuce, Swiss cheese, and mayo. Fresh tomato complimented the grains and seeds in the bread. Too fast the sandwich disappeared. Licking the last of crumbs off his finger, he sighed in contentment and let serenity wash over him.

"Hey lardo," a voice said. Jacob didn't need to look across the stream to see who the voice belonged. Billy and his gang. The irony that Jacob's bully happened to be named

Billy did not escape him. Every bully had some jock name and Billy always seemed to be either the leader or member of a gang member.

Jacob looked up when the sound of splashing sounded in his ears. Horror went through him as he watched Billy and his two cohorts cross the stream awkwardly. Marcus and Zeek were with him and the trio made short work of the ankle-deep water.

"Now lookie here," Billy said to his friends. "Got my shoes all wet."

Jacob stayed sitting on the log, perched and ready for whatever torment headed his way. He could have tried to run, but the three jocks would only punish him more.

Each older boy took to their callings as captain of different teams. Zeek happened to be the swimming captain. The skinniest and most dark-skinned, the boy hated as the fastest swimmer. Marcus led the running team. Slim and pale with red hair. And Billy, the captain of the football team. Tall broad shoulders, Billy took the title of biggest in the school with no close rival.

"Yeah, me too," Zeek said. The boy was shaking his pants off.

"There's a bridge," Jacob said. He didn't know why though. The boys wouldn't appreciate the offer of information.

"What was that fatso?" Billy said walking over to him and confirming his intentions.

"There's a bridge," Jacob offered once more, but the jock just walked up to him.

Grasping him by the shirt and pulling him up, Jacob tried not to flinch. Billy wore a sneer on his face and it made Jacob fail in his effort.

'Why didn't you say so earlier?" Billy yelled at him.

Jacob stammered but his reply never got out. Instead, Billy's fist smashed into his face. Pain flash immediately into him and by instinct, Jacob went limp.

"He didn't even fight back," Billy exclaimed. Another fist fell upon him and Jacob lost his will to stand. He collapsed and Billy not understanding what happened fell atop the larger boy.

"Gross," Billy cried out in disgust. "Help me up."

Jacob felt the weight of Billy leave. He rolled to sit up but the wind rushed out of him as a foot slammed down onto his stomach.

"Did you hear that?" Marcus asked.

"Yeah sounds like one of those squeaky dog toys," Billy replied.

Jacob let the blows fall on him. It happened every few weeks after all. How long the beating lasted Jacob couldn't even fathom. For him, the physical pain faded away as he sank into the dark recesses of his mind. There, he found solace in feeling like his body sank into a pool of black oil.

"I can help you," a warm voice said. He wanted to ignore it, but the words enticed him.

"Who are you?" Jacob asked. The consciousness brought sudden pain as he felt a fist fall onto him again.

"Don't speak," the voice said again. "I feel the pain too."

Jacob remained silent.

"When they leave, by the trees you'll find a white sphere. Listen carefully. If you accept my help, find it and take it home with you. Immerse in the water next to your bed before you sleep. Don't alert anyone to it or what happens."

The warmness disappeared and brought him back to reality.

"Come on guys, that's enough."

Jacob barely registered that Marcus spoke the words. Good'ol Marcus who never actually took place in anything physical when it came to the misery inflicted. Marcus did tease, which Jacob never held against his peer because words were nothing, but it did hurt that Marcus rarely put a stop to things.

"Hey man, relax," Marcus continued.

"What?" Billy said with anger evident in his voice. "You feel sorry for the fat fuck?"

"Just got homework to do is all."

"Let's go," Billy said angrily.

Jacob heard the scuffling of feet across the polished rocks that made up the beach until that turned into splashing. The laughter faded off slowly and he didn't move. A couple of times before, Billy had returned and so Jacob had learned to stay put for a bit. He waited for what seemed like hours. When he finally moved, pain laced through his body.

"Damn," he cried aloud. He already felt stiff from the bruising and welts. It took him four tries to sit up and even then he swayed as the world spun.

"Got to be a concussion," he spoke while he wheezed. Standing up equated to conquering the world, and by the time he did, Jacob became aware that the temperature dropped. "At least I can see."

Jacob moved about and picked up his pack with gratefulness that the beating hadn't been worse. He just wished it would be the one beating he would receive that week or even day. If his dad saw him in this sorry state, the patriarch's fist would dole out further punishment. Sighing, he prepared to leave when he remembered the voice.

Looking around the edge, Jacob let out an exclamation of surprise when he saw the promised orb. Picking it up, he marveled at how light it felt. Smooth as polished stone, he got the feeling looking at it that the object lacked a look of having durability. Scared to drop it, he put it into his pack, his body protesting the series of movements. Grateful to be done with it, he looked over the site sorrowfully realizing that the one sanctuary he possessed had been taken away from him. He made a final note to return for the contents of the box and then turned away from the place.

Unlike the boys who tormented him, Jacob did use the bridge to cross the creek. The path meant more steps, which his body ached with each one, but he got to keep his clothes dry. Honestly, for a beating, Jacob considered himself lucky. Sure the pain existed but the boys had left him in far better shape than he should have been in. In all honesty, as he hobbled painfully through the woods, he surmised that because today happened on a Friday, the bullies had pressing matters. Like the school dance that night. If Jacob thought correctly, he knew why Billy had come for him.

Lunch that day at school for the seniors had been busy. As peers gossiped and made final plans, Jacob had sat alone in the corner as per usual. He had already eaten, that day three snack cakes, a sandwich, and two cokes, and sat there observing. One of the things he observed was Billy being shot down for a date. The boy must have seen Jacob smirking, which to Jacob, he smirked at the small justice the universe had given.

Out of the woods, Jacob walked along a paved path, popular with runners and the like. No one used it now except Jacob. Grateful to the heavens for that small measure of luck that none would stop him from demanding to know what happened, a reason centering on bad repercussions from his father in the past, he continued as fast as he could go.

The effort paid off and by the time he reached home, the pain had dulled and his clothes were soaked in sweat. Even before he reached the street his home sat on, Jacob could smell himself. A smell that embarrassed him to no end and one he could never hope to get rid of.

Rounding the corner to his street, he saw that no one was about. No doubt as the evening grew later, everyone that lived on his block made plans for

Friday. As he walked it grew apparent to him that his father's truck didn't sit in the driveway.

"Thank you," Jacob said with a sigh of relief. He didn't want to see his father that night. Continuing on he paused in the driveway right next to the mailbox where he leaned on it.

The house that Jacob lived in sat in the center of the row of houses. It also happened to be the biggest, built for a family of at least six, but it never got to see that. Jacob looked longingly over to the flower garden where a stone cross marked the memory of his mother. A constant reminder of where everything went wrong. It reminded Jacob and his father that his birth had killed his mother over time he went into the house. His father once had told him the cross had been a prized possession of his mother's but now instead of fond memory, it brought nothing but tragic pain.

The home had five bedrooms on the second story, one of which was a massive master bedroom. Apparently, his mother had wanted to have a lot of kids and intended to do so. All of the rooms had things in them to that effect. Two boys and two girls, his dad would tell him over the years. The master bedroom sat undisturbed and his father slept in one of the empty rooms. Jacob had his room of course, and the other two rooms were untouched except for the abandoned kid's furniture projects.

A snap sounded and Jacob barely had enough time to register that the sound came from the mailbox. He stepped away as quickly as possible to see that the wooden pole now leaned and the wood cracked.

"Crap," he said sudden fear going through him. When his dad saw it no doubt retribution would come. Sullen, went up the steps of his house.

The key to the home had been hidden on the screen door right inside in one of those black magnetic key holders. Getting it out, Jacob opened the door before putting it back and going inside.

Entering into the Grand home meant entering into a view of nothing. There was no picture on the walls, barely any furniture. Most had been broken by his father in his drunken stupors. The house was a shell of what could have been. Stains on walls and wooden floors where polish and paint long since faded greeted all who entered, which for the home, often meant no one but Jacob. With a sigh, he went upstairs to his room.

Jacob would have to give kudos to his dad on a few things. One is that even though the patriarch was abusive, the man took care of his son. Jacob had a massive desk, a bed, and shelves lined with collectible items. Each section of the shelves had a designation.

The shelf next to his desk held books and notebooks. The two walls next to his bed were filled with figures. The last top to bottom had finished models and hand-painted figures. All paid for by the generous allowance his dad gave him. Jacob didn't understand how such an abusive man offered such solace, but he never questioned the stacks of cold hard cash and written notes on instructions his dad would leave. The man worked hard for some job and drank himself to a grave at night.

Jacob went to the bathroom and stripped. From there, he examined his body as much as he could in the mirror. Bruises of purple and black were shown on his skin, some brand new and others faded. He smiled a bit thinking that he could have been a furry and spotlighted as a leopard. With a shudder though, he dismissed that thought and lumbered into the shower.

During the time that Jacob entered and exited the shower, he reflected on the shower. He could barely move in the thing but did his best to wash. A process that involved lots of soap on a back washer, which he used for his whole body. When he did exit, Jacob did the one thing he promised he would never do until he saw weight loss. He stepped onto a scale.

Numbers jumped accordingly fast on the digital scale. He watched and two hundred flashed by. The scale stopped at three-eighty.

"I lost six pounds," he said excitedly with the news. "I can't believe it. I lost six pounds in a week."

Smiling now, he got off the scale and lumbered back to his room. Naked and all he walked over to his desk and sat in the chair. It protested loudly with his weight, but he hoped that enough would be lost before it buckled.

Logging onto the laptop he owned, an Apple, he searched diligently for different strategies to lose weight. Jacob had begun thinking of losing weight a couple of years ago. With no help or understanding, he realized through researching online that he was an emotional eater. All the pain he had dulled by food, but that action no longer held appeal to him, even if he couldn't escape what he did.

Portion control had been his first step. Next week he planned on walking more, but he was afraid of that. The exposure for sure meant more opportunities for ridicule. A fear that he knew that needed overcoming if he wanted to succeed.

Written on a sticky note and posted on his desk were a series of goals. The first one to lose weight. The second is to be fit. Third, kick his bullies' asses with the latter word circled. The last note just had the word Dad written on it.

Getting up from the chair, Jacob retrieved his pack. He opened it up and began taking out his school things. It wasn't until he felt something round through the interior that he remembered the sphere. Pulling it out he looked at it. It looked bigger now and felt heavier.

"What are you?" He asked it, but it didn't reply. Sighing he put it on his desk. After an hour of aimless surfing, he put a game on. That took him late the night and his stomach growled reminding him he hadn't eaten dinner. A few clicks on the computer and he ordered a specialty salad from a place he never had before. Then he got dressed and went back to playing the game.

The game took over once more only interrupted when the food arrived announced by the doorbell ringing. Jacob rushed to answer the door, getting there in over a minute.

A small petite girl greeted him when he opened the door. The kind that Jacob had dreamt about, but never would look his way. The look of surprise on her face at the sight of him told him everything he needed to know about how he looked. He gave her some money, a tip included and took the pizza from her. She said nothing to him and him to her as he went back inside. Sad now, he ate the salad in the kitchen. After he finished, he got a glass of water and headed upstairs having decided that bed would be better than continuing to be awake.

Back in his room Jacob put the glass of water on his nightstand and went to his desk. Grabbing the white sphere, he walked back over to the glass of water.

"I wonder what will happen," he said aloud before shrugging. He dropped the sphere into the cup of water you said was big. But if it could be dropped inside a cup it is more like marble than a sphere. The displacement pushed up some water over the rim of the cup. He ignored it and closed the door to his room before climbing into bed. Laying down, Jacob looked at the immersed sphere and wondered what it could be. A thought that stayed on his mind as the darkness of see enveloped him.

"Jacob," a feminine voice said.

"Who's there?" Jacob replied groggily. His awareness felt murky, like being in the water. "You did well," she said.

Perception returned and he found himself in a cone of light, on the stone floor.

"What is this?" He asked.

"We are in your mind," she said. "In your dreams, while you rest."

"Who are you?"

"I have no name," she said. "A more apt question is what, but at your current mental capacity, that answer will drive you insane."

Jacob thought about that answer for a bit.

"So what do you want?"

The light suddenly brightens to push back the darkness. What was before he could only be described as a nightmare. On a throne sat a mass of writhing tentacles. He noticed how they seemed to have a feminine figure as apparent curves presented themselves.

"Relax human," she said. "I don't mean you any harm and you need to process what you see before you before we can proceed."

He breathed heavily, trying to catch his breath.

"Millennium has passed without me revealing myself to anything on a mortal plane of existence," she said. "Gods have been on your plane, and even some Old Ones."

He shook with fear but focused on the tentacle that looked to be the head of the thing. Everything looked slimy and pink.

"So what do I want human besides you?" She asked. "I want to be tethered to the world and to do that I need you. A pathetic human to be molded and bonded to me into a perfect mate."

"Why?"

"To be loved by someone unconditionally. I want to be your everything when it concerns all matters. Be that as a motherly figure, a lover, a protector, and most importantly, I want a mate."

Jacob looked to her, his mind adjusting to the writhing mass of tentacles. He thought to himself that her appearance, while alien, couldn't be that bad. Something inside told him though that even if he had an issue, it wouldn't matter. A monster could get what it wanted.

"Why not Billy or anyone else?"

"Because you, my boy," she said. "Are going to help me conquer the world and to do that, I need a devoted mate who will worship with me in all carnal delights."

"You want to have sex with me?" 'And many other things.

His mind had a hard time understanding what she offered.

"Are you a god?"

"No, but soon you will think so if you accept me."

"What do you mean?"

"We have to accept each other, which means we have to meld together in passion. Not only for me to be born, but to praise our goddess."

He swallowed hard and found that he had a lump in his throat.

"All you have to do is say yes and it begins."

"Who is the goddess?"

The tentacles swirled around while they writhed.

"She does not wish to expose herself to this world yet. We will work together to bring her glory to this place."

Jacob look stocked in everything she had said.

"I'm not a man," he said plainly. (doesn't he have a dick?)

"No, far from it actually," she said.

It hurt him.

But I will make you one fairly quickly.

"I don't know what to say," he offered after a moment of silence. He held his hands up in his defense.

"Say yes," she said with fierceness in her voice that made him jump. Not a person to resist when commanded, Jacob answered by instinct to protect himself.

"Yes."

Like a flower opening up, the trenches pulled away to reveal a woman sitting in front of him. The sight took Jacob's breath away. She looked breathtaking with her naked body. Mammaries bigger than he had ever seen with curves that oozed sexuality. Jacob had never seen a naked woman before in person, or rather in his dreams.

"You're gorgeous," he said with a whisper. She smiled at him and it made him feel relaxed and warm. To him, it seemed like a smile he had in a distant memory of his mother. Then he noticed her eyes.

Her eyes looked like the night sky. Hues of blues and blacks dotted with white dots. Pink skin and white teeth. There was no discernible nose.

"Is this what you will look like?" He asked.

"No," she said. "I will have to bond with your essence to take form on your plane of existence. As such, I will take on characteristics native to your kind."

"Are you okay with that?"

Her eyes didn't reveal anything to him.

"Boy, we have talked too much and I grow impatient now. You have accepted the terms, now come to seal them."

The alien creature before spread her legs and Jacob looked aghast at what unfurled in front of him. Jacob had seen women naked on the internet. He knew what a pussy looked like, but what she presented between spread legs twisted around. Then the tentacles spread like a flower.

"I hope you like the view," she said. "Now come seal the deal with a kiss upon it."

Dream or not, weird nightmarish monster or not, Jacob's mind took over to obey her on command. Practically running over, he knew in front of the throne and leaned forward.

"What is your name?" He asked hesitating once at the moment of really kissing the sex of the being. The tentacles twisted in front of his face. He scantly heard her answer, which sounded like complete gibberish, as his eyes wandered over the slimy-looking sex. There were folds, but little to tell him that it was sex. The tentacles could have acted like labia, but then they show out and wrapped his head.

Jacob struggled especially when his face became pressed up against warm and wet.

Jacob breathed and took in the musky scent, which as he panicked, made him realize that nothing bad would happen. As he relaxed, it felt like the tentacles were barely holding him. Relaxing, even more, he did what she wanted.

He pressed his face willingly now into her sex. Her directions were to seal the deal with a kiss, so that is what he did. A smooch onto her sex, but it left his lips covered in slime. Tasty and sweet slime that mimicked him, honey. Jacob could do sweet and so he licked her sex much like he would an ice cream cone. Tentacles relaxed and the cool air barely registered to him.

"Stop mortal," the woman commanded, but he didn't. Kept licking and making lewd slurping noises. "Come on Jacob."

A hand planted itself on his head and pushed him back.

"What's wrong?" He asked with alarm in his voice.

"I appreciate your eagerness to for worship, but without a physical body, I won't feel anything."

Jacob's eyes dropped in disappointment. He felt that her offer should have been met with enthusiasm and maybe, just maybe, make him feel like he had done something right. She hadn't felt anything.

"The terms are accepted," she said. Jacob looked up at her to see that her arms and tentacles pointed upwards to the sky. He looked up to the source of the light above and it blinded him.

Blinking heavily, he briefly wondered how such a dream could be possible. Everything going on here the question that needed to be answered is why he hadn't woken up yet. Hearing movement, he blinked his eyesight clear. Looking up at her, they locked eyes.

"Are you ready to give me the form?"

He swallowed. Had no idea what she meant. The smile on her face though unnerved him. That smile scared him. A look that said he was about to have his whole life change.

"Yeah," he said with a whisper.

Two things happened at that moment. The first, the woman dropped in front of him and grasped his face. The second is that he felt suction on is groin.

Don't move," she said. "This process is delicate.

"What are you doing?" Jacob said with a shudder. The sucking had grown pleasant around his cock.

"I have to join you."

"What does that mean?" he said with a moan.

"Joining requires an exchange of fluid between us. You took mine into you, now I have to take yours in."

"But this is a dream," he said with a sudden inflection in his voice. He felt like he was buried in something. Maybe it felt like an actual vagina. All he knew is that even in the dream, his cock felt like it had crossed from virginity into blissful manhood.

"It may be a dream," she said with a whisper. "But outside of your mind, I am currently attaching to your body. The suction you feel is happening."

"Then why this?"

"Because I don't need you to move or wake up. That would ruin the joining."

"Like a parasite?"

She laughed.

"Yes," she said.

His release took him by surprise and the world around him began to shift. He moaned as he began to awake.

"Hush now Jacob," she said in the dream and the world began to re-solidify. "Remain her with me."

"What's happening," he said.

"I am absorbing as much as I can right now."

Jacob felt weird. His whole body tingled and his head swam.

"This is just a dream," he said aloud. It wasn't clear to him if the effort convinced him that he would wake up with nothing changed in his life. Though if she promised such pleasure, he hoped his life would change.

"You taste good," she said. "But I'm not big enough to eat so much."

He didn't know what she meant. He just knew as he sat in front of her that for the first time in his life, he was relaxed.

"What-" he spoke, but no thought could be completed. As he tried to focus, the monster woman had gotten up and sat back on the throne.

"Get some rest, my servant," she said with a smile. "Soon the carnal delights will be physical."

His vision blurred and the world went to the color black. No dreams or thoughts until something slamming woke him up.

"Jacob!" a stern male voice shouted.

Adrenaline shot through his body as he stumbled to get out of bed. He looked at the clock to see red numbers showing three-fifteen.

"Jacob!" his father yelled once more. Even panicked, Jacob realized he wasn't wearing any pants. Fumbling around, he found a pair quickly and put them on.

"Yeah dad," he called back.

"Get your ass down here," his dad shouted back at him.

Tired, Jacob couldn't even muster an eye roll as he went to see his father. To him, the annoyance of the man every weekend always started in the early morning with a drunk scream like this one. It also always ended with some sort of beating too.

Sleep drifted away fast and by the time Jacob made it down the stairs to see his father, he felt strangely alert. Most of the time when he walked into the living room where his father would be sitting in an old recliner, he felt groggy. Now, as he stepped into the living, Jacob realized then just how bare it was.

A single TV stand and a couch were the only things in there besides the recliner. A thought occurred to him about actually filling the room up with things. There happened to be a monthly allowance that never got used for anything except his room. Funny how that never occurred to him before.

"What took you so long?" His dad demanded. It's how the conversation always started. A comment about how slow he moved.

"Sorry da-," Jacob went to reply.

"Don't be," his father said.

A slurp sounded and then Jacob realized the two of them weren't alone. On her knees in front of his dad was a woman with her back towards Jacob. Jacob blushed to realize that the slurping meant the woman currently had her lips wrapped around his father's cock.

Only once had such a thing ever occurred and that time he hadn't seen anything. He could see now as eyesight adjusted to the darkness of the room, that she was naked.

"God Sean, what the hell?" She said.

"Go back to what you were doing," his dad said. The edge in his voice gave a clear warning that he would be unhappy if she didn't listen. Still, she didn't look back before the slurping continued.

The man had no patience. Jacob looked down on his father even five feet away and still would if the man stood up. Sean Grand had a mean right hook but suffered in height to his son. That height didn't hinder the man either when it came to women. A drunk or not, Jacob's father could pull some "Tail," as the man put it.

"You lose weight?"

The question was random, and in fact, not something he expected his father to comment on.

"Yeah."

Jacob expected his father to stand up and swing on him then. The man always demanded to be called sir. Instead, a moan emitted from the man.

"Deeper," Sean said.

Whoever the woman was, she audibly gagged on his father's cock.

"I'll be gone for a week or more," the man said after a few moments. Jacob hadn't dared walk off at least to spur any wrath. Standing as motionless as possible, even holding his breath for long periods. He heard his father moan and the girl responded to it with a sultry one of her own.

'Yeah, you like that huh?" Sean said.

"Mmhmm," she responded with a long sucking noise.

"Having an audience just gets you off doesn't it?"

There was a pop.

"Yes, daddy."

"If you like it so much, why don't you say hi?"

The woman stood up and turned around.

"Hey there," she said.

Almost speechless at the sight of his first woman, Jacob stuttered out a greeting. She didn't say anything back and he couldn't see her face.

"Jesus Shawn," she said after the moment of awkward silence. Jacob couldn't see what the two were doing, but he saw the silhouettes of them moving.

"Oh Sean," she cried out suddenly. It made him jump but he watched fascinated as she sat down on his father's lap.

"Oh yes," she grunted.

Jacob's eyes began to adjust more in the dark. The detail emerged of the woman, but her frame hid his father still. Whoever the woman was, the lack of curves looked apparent as she bounced up and down. Now Jacob began to sport a boner, but he ignored his desire.

She breathed heavily as the sex continued. A moan escaped her lips every few moments. Either for a measure or actual pleasure, Jacob didn't know. But every few seconds he saw her mouth agape in what looked like an expression of horror on her face.

Their slapping bodies made him quince each time it echoed in the room. No matter to him though, for he wouldn't raise a complaint. If he did, the scene would end and so would the small measure of pseudo-peace.

"Gonna cum," his dad cried out.

"Yes daddy," she joined him in the cry, her voice almost a shriek. "Give it to me."

The animal grunts that resounded in the room from the copulation almost made him smile. Smiling had to be controlled on his face. Anyone saw any enjoyment on his face, they took that as an invitation to ruin it. Plus, interrupting his father's enjoyment would be detrimental.

"Come on daddy, give it to me," the girl begged.

"Argh shit," his father called out in reply. The girl had stopped bouncing and instead just sat in his father's lap.

"So hot," she said. He saw her wiggling her hips as she milked his father.

"Up," Sean said, breaking the serenity of the moment.

The girl got up and scurried off past Jacob. A hand covered her face as she went by. He caught a whiff of perfume mixed with sex, but he also so that her eyeshadow ran in longlines down her face.

Got to run into another state for work.

"Okay sir," Jacob said, his focus back on his father He did his best to avert his gave to the man but couldn't. He thanked the heavens his father though could barely be seen in the dark.

"I'll leave money for you of course," he said. It was customary that his father established there was money available.

"Thank you, sir," he said as he usually did to the "gift."

"You need to get a job soon."

Those words sent dread through Jacob and changed the direction of the conversation. He would never be able to get a job. Not with the way he looked.

"If you keep losing weight, sure someone would hire your worthless ass."

If his mother could have been there, maybe she would have said something to her husband about the words. Then again, maybe his father would never have said them to begin with.

"You should thank someone when they compliment you."

"Thank you, sir," Jacob spat out fast and as sincerely sounding as he could muster.

"Go back to bed," his father said. "I'll be gone in the morning."

Scared to move, Jacob froze. His father rarely let him leave without more verbal and physical abuse.

'You need to be told twice?" His father yelled at him.

"No sir," Jacob said turning on his heel and fleeing the room. As he left he found the girl still naked sitting on the stairs. Pausing, he decided to risk getting her a glass of water.

Rushing to the kitchen, Jacob got a glass of ice and poured a glass of water using one of the many water bottles in the kitchen. Quickly he returned to the woman and handed her the glass. She accepted and he walked passed her as he went up to his room.

Up the stairs and into his room, Jacob closed the door behind him and had an alien feeling that he moved much farther than he should have.

"What's going on?" He said aloud to himself. He looked at his bed and saw that the glass of water on his nightstand had fallen over. Rushing over, he looked over the stand to see no water had spilled. He looked under the bed and couldn't find the smooth rock either. Confused, he stood up and felt something heavy hit his inner thigh.

"What was that?" He asked. Pulling down his pants and trying to look was a useless endeavor. The enormity of his stomach kept him from seeing his groin. Thinking, he decided the bathroom mirror was the best thing to use to see what was going on. Heading to the bathroom, without his pants on, Jacob wasted no time looking in the mirror.

To his horror, there was something attached to his groin. He locked eyes with a single eye that matched one of the alien-looking women in his dream. The thought that the dream woman's words of carnal delights and changes replayed in his mind once more. What if the whole thing happened to be a ruse? Jacob wanted to seek help to get the things attached to him removed.

Just having an unblinking eye looking in the mirror and locking eyes with him was disturbing enough. It also hung on him like a cock sleeve and it only looked to be about three inches big.

"I need help," he said. He couldn't go to his father or the woman. That man would ridicule him somehow about the irony of Jacob willingly giving up the only sexual thing besides his hand. In fact, Jacob knew his father would give him a hard time saying anything. And who knew how the woman would react? Better to be happy getting some his dad would say. Then the thing visibly pulsed and grew bigger. A pressure also grew on his cock.

The eye closed slowly and the pulsing began in earnest. Jacob shook within seconds as the pleasure went through his body. Having to lean back against the bathroom wall, he almost couldn't move as his knees buckled. Looking out into the hall, he managed enough strength to close the bathroom door. By the time it closed and he looked back to the mirror, an orgasm ripped through him.

Fascination went through him as he breathed heavily to recover. The parasite on his cock had grown a bit in girth. It looks fatter and then it grew longer. The eye opened back up and Jacob no longer felt panicked. His eyes drooped in sudden exhaustion and like a zombie; he lumbered back to his room. Falling on his bed, sleep overtook him quickly, but he didn't register that he was asleep.

The throne sat once more in front of him. Golden and covered in jewels. He hadn't noticed before how splendid the throne looked. Though in the last dream the tentacles are all his mind wandered over.

"Hello," he called out after a moment. There wasn't an answer and so he went to the throne and sat down on it. Even though the thing had no cushion, he found the seat comfortable. Sitting back he nodded his approval and marveled at how regal he felt. There was power here and he registered then that he wanted that power. Then he heard a moan.

Hello?

Oh, Jacob, you've returned.

Out of the darkness she took form in front of him. Still, a mass of tentacles but the sight of her naked breasts and spread sex made him shudder.

"Like what you see huh?"

He nodded.

"You've gotten bigger."

"I know," he replied. "I have a problem."

"I'll say," she said with a giggle that confounded him. "By the time I'm done with your cock, it's gonna be huge."

He blinked and then blinked again. A tentacle reached out and caressed his cheek.

"I didn't mean your weight there Jacky boy," she said. The tentacle was from her arm and that disappointed him. His mouth watered in want of licking her sex once more. "Though I'll say feeding on you has been tasty and informative. Your kind DNA traits are exotic."

"You're feeding on me?"

"I told you I would early my boy. I need the mass to take form and you have enough mass for me too."

"Oh," he said.

"I'm afraid though that I need more and already it is beginning to become too cumbersome to keep sucking you off." 'What?

The look on her face to Jacob looked to be one of pure hunger.

"That is why I have decided that we will have sex in your dreams."

"What will that do?"

The look on her face changed to astonishment.

"If we have sex here, I can involuntarily make your body orgasm. Such a thing is needed for me to grow."

"Will it hurt?"

Jacob didn't know why he asked, but he often heard his dad's regal tales of how cumming too many times would leave a man aching for days.

"Not the way I plan on it," she said. "Hopefully a few nights and I will have gained enough mass off of you that I can molt."

"I have school on Monday."

She smiled and then grinned widely. He saw rows of sharp teeth and it reminded him that whatever she did molt into would probably look similar to this.

"Then we best get started," she said sauntering over to the throne.

"You won't feel any pleasure," Jacob offered in meek defense to stop her.

"Not true," she said. "I have already incorporated all of you species pleasure receptors now."

"Including a clitoris?"

"Oh human, we are gonna have so much fun," she said stepping towards the throne. "I want you to repeat what you did last time, and we will see if I've done enough with your DNA."

Jacob had no time to prepare as she climbed up the throne. Feet on the legs of the throne he looked up at her speed flower as it descended onto his face looking like a sucker fish. Drips of her hunger fell on his face.

"Do you play off my imagination?"

"We can do that later, for now, it's just me," she said.

The tentacles in her groin wrapped around his head as she settled onto his face. It was peculiar to him that the woman planted her sex not his face in such a way that could have been in a movie. Thought of anything but licking her sex quickly disappeared.

Jacob couldn't get enough once more and hoped as his tongue probed into her depths that she tasted just as sweet as she did in his dreams.

Nails dug through his poppy hair and into his scalp. A groan of pain emitted from him only to be drowned out by a moan from her. His tongue lapped around across her wet skin and it surprised him when she shook. The flesh quivered like an earthquake around him. Then he couldn't breathe as his legs squeezed around his head. By instinct, he flailed his arms and pushed against her flesh as fear of suffocation became a real reality to him. The world swam and began to shift until suddenly she wasn't on him anymore.

He didn't know when the change happened but suddenly he was alone in the dream now. Sitting confused on the throne, he wondered what had gone wrong. The darkness past the light yielded nothing.

Everything to Jacob now centered on his dick. Even as he sat in class and the hot history teacher droned on about the Civil War, it was all he thought about. How hard it was and how difficult it was to conceal. Mostly because the alien organism suckered to it.

He knew little about it except what it claimed to tell him in his dreams. The alien woman in those dreams didn't share much either. All it seemed to want is to tease him and feed off him. The results so far over the past few days had lengthened it from a mere inch to almost twelve. What weirded him out, is that it felt for him like his cock had grown with it.

Even worse, his clothes were beginning to not fit. Before, he either wore a really big pair of jeans or just stuck with sweats. He wore sweats today, but he worried the thick pole in his pants would be seen. Though with a fifty-pound weight loss so far, the clothes began to become baggy.

An open juice box of orange juice suddenly brought his thoughts from his cock when it smashed painfully against his face. A peal of group laughter sounded from the other side of the room. Of course, the perpetrators were Billy and his gang of friends. All three of them live with no regrets, and Jacob wished they would just disappear.

"Billy," Ms. Devons yelled. "Office now."

Billy laughed as well as his friends.

"Just a joke," he said shooting daggers of anger over at Jacob. Jacob knew right at that moment, that even though he lacked any blame for the situation, Billy would blame him.

"Not a joke, office now," Devons screamed. Many in the class cringed, not because of her sudden inflection but because no one talked to Billy in such a way. Boy's family had money and so far, Billy had scantly felt any consequences for his actions.

"Fuckin cunt," he said before storming out of the classroom.

Jacob said nothing and he did nothing. Mrs. Devons happened to be the nicest person in his life and he didn't want to risk upsetting her. Even if he suspected she just felt sorry for him. The interruption was dealt with, and the class continued without another problem. Except maybe that Jacob could not keep his mind once again off his throbbing cock.

When the bell rang, Jacob watched as each student filed out of the class. A ritual in which he would be the last student out. Better that way for them and him. No one had to deal with him and he could move at his slow pace. As the last student went out, he stood up from his desk and moved towards the door.

"Jacob," Ms. Devons spoke to him stopping his navigating through the desks. He turned and found she was next to him, dwarfed by his massive frame. She was smiling up at him and he saw the beginnings of crow's feet. She may be older, but Jacob thought she looked amazing.

"Yes," he said in a low voice.

"Are you doing okay?"

"Yeah," he said before turning and meandering back into the halls of the school. Thankfully the history class was the last of the day. Mostly because a boiling heat of anger had surged in the pit of his stomach. Somehow, the display of concern from Ms. Devons angered him where before he would just feel ashamed.

With a sigh, he went to the bathroom on the way out of the school. There, he urinated and washed his hands and face. Just as he prepared to leave, the heavy bathroom door opened and Billy walked in.

"Well, well," the boy began. "Looks like I just got lucky."

"Better back off," Jacob stammered.

"What did you say, fat boy?"

"Let me be."

Billy got into Jacob's face. Normally their raised fist of Billy would have made Jacob flinch in fear.

Much to his surprise that changed to Jacob's fist smashing into Billy's face. That surge of anger finally exploded out of his belly and a satisfying crunch could be heard.

"You broke my nose," Billy screamed in pain. Jacob shoved the jock out of the way in desperation to escape. Blood dripped to the floor, which was the last Jacob saw about Billy as he rushed out of the bathroom. He even managed to run to the door of the school and went out unharassed. Out of breath, he struggled to walk but pushed himself to make it home.

When Jacob made it home, thankfully with no further incidents, he found himself craving fruits and vegetables. Thankfully his father had left him a stack of money, so he ordered Chinese. An order of mixed veggies and one meat dish. When he completed the order and hung up the phone, the Chinese guy on the other end seemed surprised. After all, Jacob never ordered less than a plate of rice, three types of meat, and often one or two appetizers.

Feeling disgusting with himself though, the sweat sticking to him and the smell, he took a shower. There, he washed and became delighted that he could turn around in the shower.

"What are you doing to me?" He asked the alien attached to his cock while he looked at himself in the mirror. As if to answer, the thing came to life and he shuddered in pleasure as it milked him. Expertly it brought him to orgasm quickly and as he shuddered in orgasmic bliss, he swore it grew another inch. He made a mental note to ask the being later about it in his dreams.

A few minutes later he was in his room looking for clothes to wear. While searching, sudden sharp pain in his crotch caused him to fall to his knees in pain. While there, tears flowed freely from his face. A sudden painful sucking began on his cock and he shook as something weird began. As he rolled around, the pain caused him to blackout.

Jacob found himself once again in the dream state place that always greeted him when he wasn't awake. He stood in the cone of light, as per usual, in front of the golden throne that the mass of tentacles sat upon. Concealed in that mass of tentacles was a goddess of sex. Or rather, not a true goddess, as she claimed to be the harbinger of her master of lust.

"What's going on?" He asked the swirling mass of tentacles and cringing as even the pain could be felt here.

"Relax Jacob," she said.

"It hurts," he replied doubling over.

"A little pain is a small price to pay for us," she spoke. Normally she would have been sultry but the voice sounded flat and focused.

'What are you doing to me?" He cried.

"I have to have mass there master. For that to happen, I have to suck it off of you. By the time I am finished, we will have made you more pliable for a male of your age."

"Why does it hurt?"

"There's a lot I have to take. We have bonded by now and let me tell you, I am so happy about that. It took me longer than expected to break down your genetic material for that."

The pain dulled for a moment and Jacob did his best to recover.

"When will you be done?"

"Because of your schedule and needs, in the next few minutes."

He let out a sigh at that.

"You said you're taking mass, at that speed won't I look skinnier than I do now?" "Extremely so," she said. "Oh, I get your point. You will have to go to the hospital then." "What?"

"After you eat of course. Just say you came home from school, took a nap, and woke up like you are."

"But," he said trying to come up with a counter-argument. That much change would surely give rise to many questions.

"Don't worry, just claim you are having a hard time and get a doctor's note explaining everything and take a few days off from school."

"I," he wanted to talk couldn't.

"And we will have plenty of time to enjoy each other with my new body and yours," she said. The mass of tentacles still swirled but they gave him no indication of when the pain flared up suddenly. "And besides, we have to work on completing me and for that, you need some time to tone your body."

And then the pain became excruciating and he felt like he was shrinking. Then as soon as it all began, the sound of a doorbell going off brought him back to the real world.

The first thing he registered was the lack of pain. The second, his cock was free. Even though he still wore clothes, another ring of the bell kept him from investigating. Getting up, he held his pants up as he made it through the house to the door. Opening yielded a surprise.

"Jacob?" That was the delivery boy named Mark. The two had known each other since the first time Jacob had ordered food.

"Yeah," he replied holding out the cash and taking the bagged food.

"What happened man? You need a doctor?"

Jacob only nodded no, before assuring Mark that he was headed to the E.R. in a few. "You have a ride?"

"No, I can call a cab," he said.

Fuck that man, you need attention now.

Jacob fed himself struggling not to comply with Mark, but the guy dragged him to his car and drove him to the emergency room.

"I'm off at eight, so if you get out before then, just wait by the bus stop over there. I'll pick you up."

Jacob watched as Mark drove away and sighed. He didn't want to do a hospital, but somehow, both Mark and his goddess were correct. Plus, what better way to get out of school for a few days and get a break? Sighing he went into the emergency room.

The receptionist was a chubby redheaded girl. She had freckles, and green eyes, and wore purple-rimmed glasses. Her lipstick matched the glasses.

"How can I help you?" She asked.

"I need help?" He said.

"Oh dear," she said standing up from the desk. "Do you have insurance?"

Jacob realized then that the women assumed he was homeless. He took out his wallet, a struggle with the loose clothes being held up, and gave her the card.

"What exactly is your issue?" She asked.

"I've lost weight," he said. "Like two hundred pounds in a couple of days."

Her eyebrows rose.

"I wouldn't be walking around in ill-fitting clothes like this if I wanted to. Here take a look at my school I.D."

She swore when she looked at it.

"Let me get you to an examination room."

Seconds later, a plethora of tests was run on him. Blood was drawn, and he was left in the room to himself. Hours could have passed, and he leaned his head back to close his eyes. He had hoped to fall asleep to chat with her once more, not even knowing if he could still. A doctor walked in.

"Jacob Grand?"

"Yes, sir," Jacob replied to the older male. The man had no hair and his head shone like it was polished.

"You've got quite a problem it seems," he said. "What happened?"

Jacob told him exactly what his goddess had told him too. The doctor didn't believe him though.

"You may have picked up a parasite," the doctor offered, and Jacob wished he could have told him that was right on the money. The problem was, that parasite had removed itself.

"Will I be okay?"

"Only time will tell. We took some blood samples so in a few days we will know for sure." "Until then?"

"I want you to be at home and avoid contact with anybody. We will know now if it is a parasite, but I honestly feel like this is a prank."

I am who I say I am," Jacob said in defense.

"I believe you, just farfetched you can lose so much weight so fast," the doctor said while looking at his clipboard. "I would commit you in, but you look fine and so far all the tests we ran say you're as healthy as a young buck."

Jacob didn't know how to respond even as the doctor gave him the excuse and left. After a moment, Jacob went out of the Emergency Room and waited by the stop at a loss. Having forgotten his phone and anything, he just sat at the stop with his baggy clothes. At least the temperature was moderate.

Minutes could have passed or even hours but he sat enjoying watching passing traffic.

No one bothered to sit with him in the enclave and no one walked by. Eventually, Mark actually drove up in his car. Jacob got in.

"Hey man, so what do they say?" Mark asked.

"Said I might have a parasite."

Jacob didn't look at Mark but peered out of the window and watched as buildings passed by.

"That isn't good," Mark offered.

"At least I lost some weight, but I have to be out of school for a few days, which works because I have to get clothes and can't be near anyone as much as possible."

"Well, if you need some help just call me here."

Mark handed over a business card to Jacob.

"Thank you," Jacob said taking the card. The gesture confused him, but he didn't say anything else as they pulled up in front of his house.

"Hey man, call me if ya want to hang sometime," Mark said to him as he got out.

"I will," Jacob said before heading into the house.

Back inside, his stomach growled, reminding him that he had never eaten. Feeling famished, he reheated his dinner and ate it. Jacob found the food was much tastier and after finishing that his massive weight loss also meant having a small stomach. Feeling full now, Jacob did the one thing he knew he never should. He called his father.

The man didn't answer. Not that it surprised Jacob. He was only supposed to call in an emergency and those calls never happened. After leaving a message explaining what had happened, Jacob decided to head to bed. Early or not, he hurt and he had been through much in the day.

Falling into bed, he heavily sighed realizing he needed to order new clothes. Getting up with a heavy sigh, he sat at his desk and for the first time, didn't cringe. The chair let out no protest to his weight and it brought a smile to his face. Logging into his computer, Jacob began researching clothes.

Quickly he realized he had no idea what size he was. Feeling braver than normal, he went into his father's room and tried on a pair of pants. Those almost fit, but they were still too big at a size thirty-eight. After trying on a shirt, he found a large to fit correctly. Armed with this knowledge, Jacob ordered a whole new wardrobe from an account he had for savings.

Being one for graphics, he ordered shirts, mostly black with designs on them. Then there were the band shirts. Something he had always wanted to wear, but never possible due to the lack of size variety. Feeling accomplished, he sat back in his chair and let out a sigh.

'Amazing how you creatures work," a feminine voice said.

Jacob looked around his room in a panic.

"You've forgotten me already?" She replied with a giggle.

"Where are you?" He asked.

"Hiding."

"Why?" Jacob asked shifting around in his chair to study his room. His eyes traced over every surface with no luck in finding her.

"Because I am terrified," she said.

"Of me?"

"I am vulnerable right now," she said. "With being attached, my metamorphous made my new body soft."

"I'm soft," he said, not quite sure why.

"Not too much anymore after me," she said with an amused laugh.

"Will I be okay?" Jacob asked with a growing pit of dread in his stomach.

"You should be, but there will be a lot more changes yet to come to herald the good news of our lady."

Jacob sat in silence for a bit debating on how to press her for more answers; especially her refusal to reveal herself.

"What other changes?" He asked.

"Well, for one, us. We need to join together soon, but my skin has to finish hardening." "Are you gonna feed on me more?"

"I can't," she said after a moment of silence. "Your body can no longer provide what I need to continue my evolution."

"What do you mean?"

"I need a woman to get the chemical and hormones my body needs to become more humanoid."

"So you don't look like that right now?"

"Patience, Jacob."

"What are the other changes?"

"I would think you would admire the gift of the cock I gave you."

She was right about that. Even sitting in the chair, the alien feeling as it lay placid on the edge of the chair. He worried a bit.

Sighing, Jacob got out of his chair and shut off his computer. Silence returned and he moved around the room turning off lights and all. He gave a pause in his doorway before he closed it; listening for a phone ring he knew would never sound. With a sigh, he closed the door to his room and flipped the light off.

In bed, Jacob let his mind wonder about things. For one, he wondered if he fell asleep would his dreams return or would it be a marathon of sex?

Strangely he thought about his father for a bit. Would the man even care about the weight loss?

Sighing, he tried relaxing before falling asleep. His mind, though, had different plans. Fear went through him suddenly as he realized the repercussions of the pact now. The amount of questioning that would be sure to follow after everyone saw him made him breathe heavily. What would everyone think?

When something rubbed against his foot, he let out a yelp of surprise. He shifted quickly and pulled himself up to the head of the bed until he was sitting and could go no further. Suddenly his blanket rose.

"Relax Jacob," she said.

"Christ you scared me," he replied noticing that her rise had stopped.

"I am ready," she said. "Turn the light on."

Jacob obeyed and flipped the lamp on his nightstand next to the bed. Blinking heavily by the sudden brightness he wondered briefly about what was about to happen. If she re-attached to him or even what she looked like made his imagination run wild with fear.

"Pull the blanket off," she commanded after a second. At that moment, gripping the fabric of the comforter, Jacob somehow knew his old life as a fat boy that got picked on constantly would end at this moment. With a pull, the blanket came away and revealed to Jacob a serpentine body.

Pale white flesh revealed itself quickly on a coiled body. She had the shape of a snake, but the body was bigger than anything he had ever seen. He wanted to panic and run, but those galaxy eyes once again trapped him in their allure. Her face almost had some humanity in it, but only some. Long, it did look like a garden snake. The tentacles she sported for hair hung in long locks.

"Hey master," she said with a soft mewl, and he could swear she was smiling.

"Hey," he said completely confused by her look.

"I told you I need more of your species DNA to progress further," she said as a matter of fact. "While I have fashioned a receptacle to receive you into for both of our mutual pleasure, I will need a female of your species to reproduce."

"So, we can have sex?" He asked being the only thing that she offered that made sense to him."

"Yes, we can have sex," she said with a giggle. "Would you like to now?"

Jacob couldn't process the offer. A girl, well a female something wanted to have sex with him. A strange stirring happened.

"Oh, I can see you like the thought of it," She said. He thought the white specks in her eyes shimmered like diamonds in the light.

Uncomfortable with his shorts on, he took them off quickly. When his cock sprung up, he gasped.

"What did you do?" He asked in wonderment of the meat stick that rose before him. The head was purple and swollen, pulsing angrily in its need for release.

"I just teased you a lot in your dreams," she said with a lick of her lips. He saw that her tongue was purple. "And I am glad I did."

Droplets of pre-cum oozed from the tip.

"Would you mind if I tasted it?" She asked with no hesitation of decency.

His heart stopped. Never in his wildest dreams would he have thought to be asked such a thing. The way he looked before, probably wouldn't be a woman in a million years who would have looked at him. Not that the alien life form in front counted as a woman, but she identified as a girl and that was good enough for him.

"You have to grant me permission," she said. Her head swayed back and forth, mesmerizing Jacob.

"I," he began not even registering an actual thought. "Grant permission."

Suddenly a long purpled tongue was wrapped around his entire length. The pressure of it made him moan and swirled pleasurably around his shaft. Her eyes didn't leave his as she 'tasted' him. To him, it felt like that taste left nothing untouched on his scrotum. After a bit, the cool air caressed his cock once more as she pulled away.

"It's delicious," she said.

An unfamiliar feeling washed over him. Queer as it was he did speak.

"Thank you," he said watching as her hair tentacles danced. "Can I see yours?" "Certainly," she said with a squeal of delight.

He watched in fascination as her serpentine body rose. As it rose, he marveled at its smooth pale skin. It looked succulently soft and so he reached out to touch it.

Oh?" She said in surprise.

"What?" He said recoiling from her exclamation.

"I didn't think you would take such an action."

"Was I wrong?" He said suddenly afraid that he had ruined the whole thing. Thoughts of self-doubt plagued him.

"No," she said with a cock of her head. "I don't understand why you would be afraid."

"I thought I ruined it," he said burying his face into his hands.

"Ruined what?" She asked. "Every action we take that pleasures not only ourselves but each other honors our mistress."

"You liked it?" He asked in surprise. Looking up at her gaze, an amount of confidence building. Bold once more, he reached out and rubbed the creatures with an open palm. "You're so soft."

"Thank you," she said.

Even bolder now, he sat forward and used both hands to feel her flesh.

"That feels nice," she said after a few moments. The words broke the spell and he settled back. "Is it time to show you?"

He nodded.

Good.

She rose and the first inkling that Jacob got that her sex approached began with the sudden change in coloring in her skin. Where her body had a pure white tone, the sudden change began as a slight pink before it steadily became an angry red. When the color became dark red, her body stopped moving.

There, Jacob saw a slit leaking copious amounts of liquid. As he studied her anatomy, it spread apart heralding a mass of tentacles.

"It is just a shaft, but the tentacles act much like a sexual pleasure organ for me," she explained.

He could care less about what she spoke of. All that mattered is that even with its completely alien look, it looked inviting. Moving towards her and off the headboard, he moved till she sat close to his body and between his legs.

"What will you do?" She asked. His answer was to grasp one of the purple tentacles. She responded with a gasp.

As he played with the spread starfish of sexual organs, he listed to her moans. A few minutes later, she suddenly let out a scream.

"What was that?" Jacob asked finding himself spitting to clear his mouth out of the liquid she coated him with.

"That was a gift from the goddess," she exclaimed falling onto him. Her weight caused him to lean back onto the bed until he lay once again. The shift of weight surprised him.

"To think you pleasured me fully before yourself. I have truly been blessed," she heaved.

He could feel the slime of her pseudo-pussy moisture spreading across his stomach. The heat of the hit made him throb in need.

'And I've forgotten about you," she said lifting up.

His eyes rose to witness the bridge of slime from her sex lift away from his stomach. "Let's fix that," she said with a sudden determination.

She shifted around trying to free his cock which was uncomfortably trapped between their bodies, when she did it sprang up with an enthusiastic bounce. A shock of delight went through him when it slapped against her body.

"Someone is sure eager," she said. Her body lowered until the heat of her sex rubbed against the underside of his cock.

"I'll say," he said stuttering in disbelief. "You seem to have lost control of your tentacles."

"Indeed, I have," she said. To Jacob, he hoped he heard amusement in her voice. That thought quickly disappeared as the tentacles enveloped his cock.

"I can't do this for long," she said abruptly.

"It feels good," he said concentrating on the feeling.

"I know, can I put it in now?"

He couldn't respond. Even when she took the liberty of sinking her sex onto his cock, they both groaned in anticipation. The amount of pleasure slammed against his brain so hard though, that by the time she took him all the way into herself, he orgasmed.

"Oh no," he cried out filling her with spurt after spurt of cum. Nothing moved while his cock spurted.

"That was a big load," she said after he had finished.

"I'm sorry," he said.

"For what?" She spoke, and he could hear the confusion in her voice.

"For cumming so fast," he said honestly feeling dejected with the sudden expulsion.

"It's all for pleasure. We both suffer from our virginities, and you should never be upset about that. Plus, I do have a pussy designed to bring your pleasure about quickly."

"Why, if you don't need my seed anymore?"

She lay on him, her hot breath on his ear.

"Because the act is extremely fun and I will need your seed to reproduce eventually." "Oh," is all he said.

"And the vessel for that should be here sometime soon."

"What do you mean?" He asked afraid once more.

"I set up the vessel that will provide all I need to become more compatible with you as your mate." 'You are perfect now.

"I can feel that," she said and at first he didn't know what she meant, but something pulsed around his rod.

"I'm still hard," he said.

"And probably will be a lot more from now on," she said. "Why don't you get on top?" "Alright."

The two of them shifted around and soon he was on top of her.

"I didn't slip out," he said in amazement.

"My tentacles apparently don't like to give up something they like."

He smiled.

"So you have to move your body," she said after a second.

"I know, just studying your body."

Her head turned from the bed to look at him.

"Then fuck me, Jacob, and make it last longer this time."

The first pull and subsequent thrusts into her depths was slow one. Jacob hadn't ever done this activity before and he wanted to make sure it was right. Plus, all he did know about sex came from the internet and some articles he had often told that one should not mimic porn.

Is it good?" He asked after another few thrusts.

So good, please keep going," she said breathing heavily.

Encouraged, Jacob picked up the pace and found himself quickly breathing as heavily as her. Except now, moans came from her. He could feel her tentacles against his stomach and suddenly it gave him an idea.

"Hey, where are you going?" She said with a whine as he pulled out.

"I had an idea," he replied looking into her eyes. "Pull your tentacles inside."

Eyebrows or rather her eyes widened as she understood what he was getting at.

"The goddess will be pleased with this suggestion."

An almost sickening sound resounded, but Jacob ignored it as best he could. Not that it mattered. Whatever alien noise her body made, it was still a vessel of mutual pleasure.

"I'm ready," she said.

Without the help of the tentacles to guide him, Jacob found the cliche' task of finding the right angle to sink into her. Eventually, he succeeded.

"Oh crap," he said when he fully buried himself into her. He couldn't even move anymore because of overwhelming sensations.

"No, not that. Sex," She cried out.

He may be unable to move, but she did. All of the contorting and writhing of her body made her take the lead.

"Give me more," she begged. Then it stopped. Jacob hadn't even realized he had closed his eyes, but he opened them to stare into her galaxy ones.

"You aren't doing a good job, Jacob," she said.

"You're enjoying it," he said trying to figure out where he messed up.

"It isn't for me, but for us. Get your ass into gear and fuck me," she said trailing off into a whisper.

It could have been a warning, and that's what finally caused the block for Jacob to break. "You want to be fucked?"

"Yes," she said in the same low tone.

"Then take it," he said leaning his head against hers. In a jiffy, he began moving and thrusting as hard as he could.

"Yes," she hissed this time before falling back. "Goddess yes."

He grunted. The feeling of her sex could not have been anywhere near as good as a human. Though he couldn't be sure of such a thing; the fact was he felt like he was sliding into a tornado of ribbed sex.

Her thrashing became savage as their sexes blurred together at a feverish pace. As much as it stung when her flesh slapped against his he refused to let up. The encouragement of her gasps and hissing pushed him further than anything before. For the first time, in a time of many firsts, he felt compelled to give everything he could.

"Jesus," he cried out as she exploded underneath him in both scream and liquid.

"Not the right one," she replied through gasps. He knew she meant for him to praise the goddess for the pleasure she was experiencing. "But please keep going."

"No plans to stop," he said as sweat pooled in his eyes. Slamming into her, he marveled at how much of an Adonis he had become. This alien girl had freely given herself to him and at that moment, he felt the feeling of utter abandonment.

The slick sound of their sexes meeting and coming apart took on eroticism to Jacob that he never wanted to stop. Even when he glanced over at his clock and saw that more than a couple of hours had passed. By now, she had fallen silent and moved only occasionally. Jacob couldn't believe how many times she had shuddered into sweet release.

"Last one," he cried out with a final thrust into her.

She didn't reply but he grunted as his balls boiled out an eruption of liquid heat. As it tapered off, too fast this time, he fell atop her before rolling to his side. Breathing heavily, he stared into the dark of his room marveling at how well he could perform.

"The goddess will be pleased with you tomorrow," she said.

"Why not now?" He asked.

"Because it was a test." She replied before the sounds of her breathing became deep. He sighed and thought about how great he felt.

There were many things he wished to experience now. The prospect of losing so much weight meant that his whole world had changed. All of it because he had gotten his ass beat by his bullies. He blinked and then suddenly found himself opening his eyes to an insistent ringing of the doorbell.

Sitting up and blinking he shook his head to clear the fog of sleep away. He didn't even do anything but quickly find a robe and put it on; which in his case happened to be ginormous. Moving quickly, he looked to not even see the snake-like alien he had spent the night with in bed. He almost disappointingly dismissed the night's activities before as a dream, but then she said something.

"Fuck her well master and bring joy to the goddess."

He looked quickly around his room but didn't see where she resided. The doorbell rang insistently again. Rushing out of his room, he made it down the stairs and found by the time he reached the door, he wasn't out of breath. The miracle continued to him and he opened the door.

"Hello," he said in surprise to see who it was.

"Hey," she said with a pause. He looked at the blond-haired girl with blue eyes. "Jacob, was it?"

"Yeah," he said utterly confused as to why the woman his father forced to fuck in front of him stood right now in the doorway. "What can I do for you?"

"I know showing up is irregular, but I need to talk to you."

Jacob looked at the woman astonished. How could she stand in front of him saying that? There was no repulsion in her like there should have been. Had it been too dark for her to see the behemoth of a fat body that he used to possess?

"You going to invite me in?" She asked after a pervasive uncomfortable moment.

"Sure," he said still astonished that she was here. He stepped aside and she went in. The door closed quickly behind.

"Surprising how dark this place is," she said as he followed her through the house and into the living room. The room where only one chair resided. "But it smells better."

They walked into the room, her first then she twirled around once before facing him. It was then that he realized she was wearing a skirt. Especially when she got halfway into the turn and it flared up showing her bare ass.

"I don't know your name," he said plainly.

"Oh, I'm Shanda," she said.

Jacob thought it was a weird name, but she seemed nice enough. She did keep her distance from him though introducing herself, but then he didn't extend a hand.

"I can understand you are uncomfortable," she said fidgeting with her hands. "Do you know where your father is?"

Jacob gritted his teeth.

"Oh no, I just want to make sure he isn't lurking around. He can be pretty possessive and also pretty dominant," she said looking over to the chair. He followed her gaze and cringed.

"He isn't around; in another state."

"Okay great," she said, her sudden cheerfulness breaking the gloom of the room.

Jacob looked over the room once more. There wasn't much besides the chair, just a curtain that hung up to black out the daylight. It happened to be particularly old, and holes had begun allowing light to peak through the fabric. Not enough, though so Jacob turned on the light to the room.

"So what can I do for you?" He asked feeling altogether out of place in the situation. It intrigued him that she stood there in front of him. He knew that her asking about his father's whereabouts also meant she feared the man's wrath.

Shanda smiled, her teeth a perfect white. If Jacob could guess correctly, he would have said the woman fit more into being a model than anything. The way she dressed oozed sexuality, something that he found intimidating. He backed away from her to lean against the wall.

"I'm not sure why I am here," she said walking over to the chair. She ran a hand over the fabric of the thing. "The other night made me never want to see him again."

Jacob nodded as she stopped behind the chair.

"I intended actually to never come back."

"Then why did you?" He asked her feeling altogether exposed to her.

"As much as your father's behavior repulsed me," she said pausing while she looked to be thinking.

Jacob had a moment to reflect that she had continued having sex with his father while the two of them conversed. Seemed to him that Shanda liked the audience.

"But you enjoyed it," he said in accusation before she could finish. A queer expression passed across her face.

"I did, so much so that I've never cum so hard in my life," she replied nonchalantly. "I'm sorry if that surprises you. I am, after all, a self-prescribed nymphomaniac."

The moan after she said nymphomaniac made it clear to Jacob that this woman meant exactly what she said. Maybe he should have been surprised, but then he remembered his pledge and mission from the alien goddess.

"Is that why you are here?" He asked her.

She came around the chair and sat in it, legs crossed.

"I am here because, in a moment of fucked up, you decided to be decent."

"All I did was give you a glass of water," he said.

"Yes, and if I had been you I would have turned around and beat the hell out of my father."

"Fat chance of that," Jacob replied with a scoff.

"Look, I get it," she said. "Even though what he did to you was amazing for me, it isn't lost on me how messed up it was."

"He doesn't care, but he will if you're trying to apologize."

"Truth there kiddo," she said with a giggle. Her legs spread slightly. Jacob noticed it, and he noticed that she saw him notice.

"Because you kept your composure, I wanted to say sorry and thank you," she said spreading her legs all the way.

A hiss sounded between his clenched teeth as he viewed her bare pussy. The first in his life to see and it was glorious.

Seems you like the view," she said.

He did, but it took him a second to realize that his cock had exposed itself in its eagerness.

"Sorry," he stuttered out a few times covering himself up.

"Nothing turns me on more than a hard cock,' she said licking he cherry lips. "I honestly would have loved to have a father-son tryst, but as we've said, your father is a little too abusive."

Jacob was surprised someone else saw how his father behaved.

"But you're not your father," she said. "Instead of freaking out at the situation, you let him talk and even gave me a glass of water after."

"Yeah," he said, blushing slightly with the compliment.

"And you haven't called me a whore, even after I told you I was a slut."

"I can't," he said not knowing really why he couldn't. He may be looking at the blond woman who excessively wore sex like a second skin and deserved the title, but something kept him from actually saying it.

"Either way, I wanted to thank you," she said with a beaming smile. "And by thank you, I mean I want you to take your cock out a come fuck me with it."

Her brazen demand made him hesitate. Suddenly a sick feeling washed over him and somehow he knew the only way to get rid of it was to obey.

"Well," he said with sudden confidence that surprised him. "I will take you up on the offer."

The robe dropped to the floor and he heard her gasp. A sudden self-conscious feeling hit him.

"Your cock is huge," she said getting up from the chair and rushing over to him. "I have to taste it."

Jacob tried to protest, but as soon as she had grasped his cock, his concerns became rather lax with the pleasure of just being grasped.

"Can I lick it, daddy?" She said. The sheer amount of perversion in those words sent a tingle up his spine. Looking down at her, he saw her eyes glowing in fascination as they moved from his cock up to lock eyes with him. "Please?"

"Yeah," he said unfamiliar with the nonchalant tone his voice had. Detached or not, he did moan when her hot wet tongue licked teasingly over the tip.

"Now what?" He asked feeling the blood pump in his ear.

"Well daddy, what do you want?"

They stared at each other, his cock pointed straight at her awaiting mouth.

"Suck it," he said, feeling a surge of power in himself with the words.

"Okay," she said excitedly before she began to choke herself on his cock.

The bimbo took his cock in her mouth like a champ. Inch by inch she worked down her throat in sloppy gaga. Once or twice she pulled off the cock for a cough before she sucked herself back onto the meat. He marveled at how she got his cock deeper down her throat with each attempt and sighed in heavy contentment when her nose pressed up again the hair of his crotch. She went to pull off, and Jacob made his first move during the entire fiasco.

Grabbing her hair, Jacob began to use her mouth as a cock sleeve. Ramming the mass of meat in and out, Jacob only lasted a few seconds before he released a tsunami of cum directly into her stomach. He lost count at six spurts before losing the ability to stand.

He fell and barely felt the sudden cool air on it his cock. It still throbbed and shot out cum as he heard Shanda coughing in a fit. Clearing his head, he gathered himself before getting up to help her.

"Are you alright?" He asked, helping her stand.

"Yeah, just a lot," she said, still coughing.

"I'm sorry," he said leading her over to the chair. He had her sit down before getting some water. When he returned, she took the glass and drank it greedily in long gulps. Soon it was gone, and she let the glass fall to the stained carpeted floor.

"Don't be," she said finally without coughing. "Whew."

"What?"

"You were blessed hon. I thought your father was huge, but you; you have a true gift there."

"Thanks," he said.

"I mean, it's too bad you came."

"Why?" He asked. She had lifted a leg, and he could plainly see her cunt. It looked invitingly wet, and soon she had it make noises that showed that effect.

Can't you see how wet I am daddy?" She said with a moaning pout.

His cock began to spring back to life. A tingling feeling already beginning as it re-inflated.

"I want to help," he said prepared to fully do just that.

"How daddy?" She said with a whine. It bothered him a bit that she called him that, but only on the unknown expectation of how he should respond. He went with what came first in his mind.

"Well little girl," he began. "I plan to fuck you with your new favorite toy."

By now Shanda had leaned back in the chair and had her eyes closed when Jacob approached and pushed her hand out of the way with his now throbbing cock.

"What the hell?" She cried out in surprise as his cock began to spread her eager cunt open.

"What?"

"I didn't think you'd be hard again so soon," she said before moaning as he earnestly began sliding in.

"I'd like to think I'm full of surprises," he said gratefully the blond bimbo hadn't seen how large he was the other night. Something felt off about it, but as he slid up the tight snatch, that concern melted away just like his cock.

Before long, they were both grunting and moaning in unison as he pummeled her. Legs eventually wrapped around his waist and the chair pushed up against a wall; a product of his hard thrusts. A rhythmic thumping could be heard with the chair being driven against the wall.

"Oh my god daddy," Shanda shouted suddenly. Jacob held on as she convulsed in the chair. A tearing sound interrupted her groans and then the side of the refiner fell off. She went with it, sliding off his cock with a laugh.

"Damn it," Jacob said in utter fear as he knew his father would flip out over the loss of the chair.

Shanda didn't share his discontent. Instead, she opted for laughing.

"You fucked his chair apart," she laughed.

"What do I do?" Jacob asked utterly lost.

"Nothing," she said. "Now let me get into a good position and fuck me up the ass with that salami daddy."

Without missing a beat, she moved on all fours to the center of the room. She leaned down and presented her pale ass to him. The skirt fell down her body, giving him an unobstructed view of her sex. Her pussy gaped, but in contrast, her wrinkled starfish looked like it had seen its fair share of reaming.

"Remember daddy; it's really sensitive so take it slow."

Jacob couldn't understand why she told him to remember, but with a shrug, he decided his first anal experience took much more precedence over a chair. With gusto, he took his well-lubricated cock and got into position.

"Not my pussy again daddy," Shanda said. By now, Jacob became frustrated at trying to get into the anal orifice. Over time he tried, his cock shifted and he slid into her pussy. "Can I help?" "Sure," he responded with gritted teeth. He didn't really understand what she did, but he knew it involved her own fingers in her greedy snatch. It did the trick and soon he was slowly sliding into a tight orifice.

"Oh daddy," she exclaimed as he slid in. He did take it slow, even though every fiber in his being urged him to bury himself fully into the woman. He knew he couldn't get his cock fully into her snatch but something told him her ass would take it all.

"This is too much," he groaned in immense pleasure that almost had him seeing stars. Up to the hilt, she took him. "Is that okay?"

"Daddy," she whined. "Pound my ass."

The sudden change in attitude from entering her slowly to actually fucking her took him aback. That sick feeling washed over him again. Fearful, he began the movement that would turn her insides out.

"Shit," she cried out.

Eventually, the slapping of their bodies took on a more powerful sound as she began to greet his thrust. He heard the tearing of carpet, and he looked up to see that her hands had dug into the fabric, anchoring them to the floor. That was fine with him, and he continued his ministrations realizing that her screams egged him on.

Jacob had never felt so alive before. Sure, last night with the alien goddess was great, but she wasn't able to move as Shanda could. Now he understood her meaning when she had told him the sex wouldn't be the same until she had a better body. Now Jacob understood and he wanted more.

The orgasm that came burning out of his cock took his breath away as he emptied into Shanda. He heard her make a weird noise but that became drowned out as the high of orgasmic release washed over him. A rush of stress was gone and a content relaxation took the pleasure's place.

When the fog cleared, Jacob saw that Shanda was vomiting onto the carpet. By now, she had pulled herself off his cock and had crawled a few feet away. Jacob fell to the floor and found himself unable to move or help her.

He saw the serpentine form of his alien goddess slither into view. "You've done well," she said to him. Her galaxy eyes now glowed blue. "I'll take her from here. Make sure I am undisturbed while I work on her. In less than a week Jacob, we will be joined."

He watched in a morbid fascination as she suddenly wrapped herself around the girl. A blink and the alien moved the girl to the stairs. Another blink and he was left in utter quiet. In a few seconds, whatever the paralysis was wearing off, he sprung up worried about Shanda.

Jacob found that neither was in his room. His father's room yielded no sign also. With fear, he went to his abandoned parent's room and found himself greeted by something his mind had no idea how to comprehend.

There, in the corner next to the bed, was a sack of flesh secured to the wall. It pulsed in weird colors and tendrils snaked away from it across every surface. He fell to the floor, realizing that somehow, Shanda no longer existed.

The dream shifted around like oil on top of the water. Jacob felt the swirling, nauseating him as he spun in it. He didn't grasp what was going on. Even as he cried out in frustrating terror, there wasn't anything he could do. Nothing worked for him.

Falling asleep had become an utter nightmare for him. From watching as the alien snake took Shana, to being terrified of the pulsating cocoon in his parent's shabby room, Jacob found himself alone. For three nights he had lain exhausted in bed, confused as to what his life had become.

When he did wake in the morning, it was to a blaring alarm. With a groan, he rolled over in bed and groggily walked through his room to the bathroom. There, he relieved himself before getting into a cold shower.

Sleep dissipated rapidly under the torrent of frigid water. With a twist of a knob, the water quickly turned hot and he relaxed a moment before washing himself. As his mind cleared, he became increasingly aware that his first day of school in almost two weeks started today. A sudden nervousness grew in him and so he tried to think of other things.

The cocoon in his parent's room only came to mind. An alien-looking thing for sure, he hadn't gone into the room since it had hissed at him two days ago. As curious as he was, he didn't investigate due to the possibility of unknown dangers.

Finished with his shower, Jacob completed a new routine for his morning. Got dressed in fresh clothes, ate a healthy breakfast, and packed his book bag. He remembered to get his doctor's note that specified today's return. At least the doctor cared. Everyone else had abandoned him. His dad was late coming home, and the alien had forsaken him to become whatever horror it wished. With a sigh, he escaped his home and headed for school.

Silverton High wasn't in any way shiny for its name. Even when one walked past well-manicured lawns and up polished concrete steps, the sole lustrous thing in the place were the trophies that greeted the students in a massive display case right in front of the doors. On each side of the case was a door to the main office, which Jacob chose to use the door on the left. Thankfully no one paid mind to him as he walked through the crowds at the entrance.

The high school's age was evident in the main office. Built years ago, everything in the office was stained dark as the wood took up almost every seeable surface. The giant counter that greeted anyone looked like a clerk counter one would find in a courtroom. Six openings allowed for school officials to talk to students or parents but currently,

these were all taken. Jacob leaned against a wall and grimaced as the bell rang signaling the start of class. His hope had been to be seated in class before anyone recognized him. Now, he would have to walk in with all eyes on him.

"Next," a voice called out.

Jacob walked up to the only opening passing a woman who looked disheveled. As he walked up, he saw etched on a golden plaque on the right of the opening the name Grace. The red-rimmed blonde peered up at him. She had emerald green eyes and red shiny lipstick on. To Jacob, Grace looked young enough to pass as a high school student and the reaction in his groin surprised him. He couldn't identify a time looking at a girl or anything in that matter out in society had elicited a response. Becoming aware quickly of how the tightness in his pants increased, Jacob smiled.

"Hey there," she said. "I don't think I've seen you before."

That stung, and he winced with those words. She didn't seem to notice, and he kept the smile on his face.

"Yeah, you have," he said. "It's me, Jacob."

His voice couldn't have been any meeker if he tried.

"Jacob Grand?" She asked with surprise evident in her voice. He saw her stand and take off her glasses before cleaning them. Once back on she let out a squeal of surprise. The whole office had gone quiet with noise. He apologized, and everyone continued to stare at him.

"Come around quick," Grace told him, but he didn't really hear her. People were staring at him. Each glare a dagger into him, a reminder of how his presence had interrupted

the day-to-day dealings of the office. Feeling exposed, he moved quickly to the side where Grace authorize him to go behind the counter. She ushered him into a side room.

"Are you really Jacob?" she asked him.

He pulled out his doctor's excuse and held it out to her. Right now, he wanted to escape the room and subsequently the school. Besides, now that he was isolated with a woman in a conference room, his nerves began to get the best of him. She accepted the note from him and read it. While she did, Jacob drank in the sight of her trying to calm his shaking.

Before, he could only see the blonde had her hair over her ears and the red-rimmed glasses shielding her green eyes. Closer now, he could see that underneath, her hair was dyed jet black. Long and straight the tips of it went past her breasts. Breasts that were concealed by an ornate white blouse. The ornateness was evident in the sewn patterns.

The blouse went down and he followed its gigue line until it changed into a black skirt. The skirt was short and there was scant bare skin as that showed she was wearing stockings. Polished black shoes were on her feet, but her legs enticed him.

"Ahem," Grace said getting his attention. His eye snapped back to her. "My, I can't think of a time the massive Jacob would dare be seen checking a girl out."

He felt the heat rise in his cheeks at getting caught. The rightness of her statement exposed him to a feeling of embarrassment he wasn't used to.

"I uh," he started.

"Don't worry about it kiddo," she said with a gleeful laugh. "It's surprising is all. What happened?"

Her nonchalant dismissal of his staring dalliance made him feel for a second like he should tell her what happened. Something told him that it wasn't the time to. "I don't know," he replied. Trying to stop to keep his voice steady and from failing. "Just woke up like this one morning. Doctors couldn't tell me and kept me out of school for the past two weeks." A gaze swooped all over his body. He got the impression of being sized up.

"I hope it's permanent," she said, and then she suddenly blushed. "I'm sorry, I shouldn't have said that."

A compliment, even if it needed to be taken back, hit him in a queer way. Receiving praise from a woman for the first time in his entire life sent a shockwave of confusing emotions through him.

"At least one thing is still massive," she spoke. He looked at her and saw a look of amazement on her face as her jaw slowly dropped. Then realized her gaze was on his crotch.

"Class," he stammered out suddenly to get control of the situation. The office was just a door away. "I have to get to class."

"Do you?" she said with a lick of her lips. Jacob saw the sudden onset of wanton lust in her eyes. Unfortunately for him, he realized the situation did need to end for both of their sakes.

"Yes," he said.

"Very well," she said with a look of disappointment on her face. "Let me get you a pass and call your teacher."

She got up off the chair and went to leave the conference room. "What's your teacher's name?"

Jacob thought for a second before he responded.

"Ms. Clemens," he replied naming the Biology teacher.

"Bet she'd like to examine you," Grace replied before walking back into the office. The double meaning wasn't lost on Jacob and the throbbing of his cock was beginning to become unbearable.

Sitting in the room for the moment, he struggled to direct his thoughts from being sexual. Three days of abstinence had been unbearable ever since the alien had awoken it. Shaking in frustration, he waited until Grace came back into the room, the massive door shutting behind her. "Well, here's your note," she said holding it out to him. Jacob took it tentatively trying not to touch her hand. She threw that out the window for him when she was suddenly up in his personal space. "This piece of paper is my number."

He couldn't move as her hand shoved the piece of paper into the pocket of his pants. She aggressively rubbed the length of his cock through the fabric of his pants. "I don't typically do direct," she said. "But we are close enough in age where you need to contact me when you can."

"I will," he said trying to relax.

"Now get to class Jacob," she said. "I am genuinely disappointed that we couldn't get better acquainted right now."

Then she was gone, and Jacob let out a sigh of relief. Feeling constricted, he waited for a few seconds to get his throbbing cock to dissipate. After thinking of his dead mother, his dick did soften.

Walking out of the conference room through a side door, he found himself thankfully in empty hallways. The walk to Miss Clemen's class took him only a few seconds, and when he arrived he again found himself panicking.

What would everyone say when they identified him? His thoughts reeled on that one question and after five minutes he almost drove himself mad trying to work the nerve up to go in. With a major sigh, he took the plunge and turned the knob.

Miss Clemens had been talking when he walked in. Standing at the board, she was wearing a red pantsuit that hugged her curves. Her ass looked amazing, but his thoughts couldn't stay on that for long. She was quick to comment on staring and often had presented herself as a purveyor of chastity. Jacob had long suspected that the woman enjoyed the stares. He did know for certain she loved to chastise the boys when caught.

"Can I help you?" she said walking briskly over to him after getting up from her desk. He kept his eyes locked on her blue ones as she walked up to him.

He held out the note to him which she snatched. Jacob seized the second while she read to look over to his classmates, all staring back in earnest curiosity. Not that they didn't know him, but his lumbering frame was no more.

"Take your seat," she said after a moment and that was that. Jacob walked to a seat at a table and she was at her desk Evidently everyone was doing textbook work and she had been giving instructions when he walked in. Textbook work was something that Jacob would know easily before completing.

Even though most students occupied personal single-seat desks, Jacob never fit into one of them. As such, the school had forced him to sit at a designated table provided in all of his classes. Today he triumphantly sat in one. Taking out his book, he looked to the board where the instructions for the day's assignment had been written.

No one seemed to care about him and after the class ended. Jacob had been apprehensive as soon as the bell rang. His following class, History, meant that he would have to deal with Billy. Sighing, he moved out of the classroom, with no harassment from anybody.

In history, Jacob took the chance and sat at a desk. As the class filled and Billy came in, Jacob hoped no one would call attention to him.

"Mr. Hayes," a student called out. "Who's this kid?"

Hayes, an older man who was chubby and balding, came into the classroom to investigate.

"Who are you?" Hayes asked. Jacob felt totally exposed but since he would have to respond, he stood up. "Jacob," he said.

There were a few audible gasps in the room as students began recognizing him. Hayes squinted at him.

"What happened?" Hayes asked.

"Lard ass got liposuction," Billy cried out. The class laughed, but Jacob stood unmoved by it, as he usually would. Something snapped in him, though. Before there would have been shame turning him to stone, but now, anger rose in his chest. A feeling that never had been present before. "Yeah, from your mom's lips," Jacob said turning slowly and defiantly to Billy. He had said it when the laughter had begun dying down.

"What did you say, fat boy?" Billy screamed angrily. Jacob noticed Hayes had backed away a bit.

"I said," Jacob issued his retaliatory statement once more. "Your mom sucked all the fat off me through my cock."

The class may have completely died down after Billy screamed, but now they were roaring in laughter. Billy wore an expression of astonishment.

Jacob turned back when the bell sounded and sat back at the desk. With his beating heart, he took out his book, and Hayes had to wait until the class ceased in their laughter before the class could begin.

History happened to be something Jacob did enjoy thoroughly. So much so, that he had already the textbook from front cover to back a few times this semester at school. These facts left Jacob quickly bored as the teacher droned on. Hayes maintained a monotone voice which made it difficult to stay awake for class, Jacob began drawing in a private notebook he had. Begrudgingly slow, the bell ending class finally rang and Jacob was out of the class quickly.

He found himself in broad halls and moved through them trying to get away from the history class as fast as possible. He had forgotten about his frame briefly as his fear overran him. Bumping into people and getting angry comments, he moved through the halls clumsily towards a cafeteria.

Inside the cafeteria, Jacob found a corner and practically hid from everyone. His social anxiety in dealing with people eventually overloaded and he left to find the library.

The library of the high school wasn't extremely big. It contained the main desk once one walked through the doors to it. Off of that, were only about thirty shelving units to support books. Not that it mattered, Jacob wouldn't be wandering through the aisles looking at the

Instead, he planned on sitting at a desk and relaxing. As he walked the librarian nodded at him and he found out quickly he was almost alone in the place. Another student wandered through the aisles and Jacob saw no one else. Going to a secluded corner, he found an empty chair and sat down in it.

The feeling of sinking into a cushioned chair without breaking it made him utterly relax. The library hadn't been an option to hide in previously with his frame. Now that weight wasn't an issue. He was content to relax through lunch before his next class.

Jacob fell asleep in the chair. As fitful as sleep had been lately, he didn't find solace in his current nap. Everything in his dream happened to be black. Various shades of black swirled like oil, but nothing took shape. His mind drifted him out in this ocean of nothingness and it troubled him.

Where was she? The alien goddess who had promised him untold pleasures and changes. Not in person or in his dreams now and it made him feel truly alone. Abandoned even. Like his mother who passed or a father who ran. Mentors who never appeared. It felt as if he should have stayed fat. At least there had been food. Then he was back in the living room, looking at himself and Shana.

Seeing both of them naked made him elated and excited at the same time. The genetic material was present, and the woman now stood ripe for assimilation. A drive of instinct pushed but a hesitation stood in the way. Her mate, its mate, wouldn't understand.

Jacob didn't understand the dream. It didn't make sense to him as he watched. His mind clicked as the scene unfolded and he realized that right now, he was experiencing the other side of the action.

He was the alien. Who hesitated in wondering if the human she had chosen as a mate would be able to handle what was about to happen? Her own basic drives though won out. A gamble for success over failure is too much to pass up.

The human woman had no idea what happened as the strike transpired. An event that needed to be quick in its execution. Any faltering could spell doom to the entire thing. As much as she wanted to keep her mate informed of the biological drives, she did not have the time to explain. With his fragile psyche, that which it was, she worried being absent from him so soon would damage him. Thankfully, she had been able to change is genetics a tad. It's how this woman had come to him. Special pheromones that enticed.

She dragged herself and the woman quickly upstairs. Already she knew the boy's room would be off limits. A pause at one door told her that the room was heavily used. It must belong to the patriarch of the place. Flicking her tongue to test the air, it was apparent to her this room's aura encompassed pain and suffering. Shanda struggled in her coils, reminding her of the lack of time. Whisking down the hall, she discovered a room that held no scents. Even though she scantily saw the furnishings, she did note that the room looked pleasant. With a finality of dismissal of it, she hauled herself up against a wall.

Shanda had begun struggling in earnest. A fact attributed to the pliability of her tender flesh. That bothered her a bit as her body currently could sustain damage easily.

"Relax," she said to the woman. When she spoke though it seemed to ignite a serious panic in the woman. She didn't know what to do, so she did the only thing she could think of.

Through her slit, a tentacle snaked out and it felt to Jacob as if he was clenching his own cheeks. The sensation was weird and he felt like he sported an erection. Instead, with her body, he knew a tentacled appendage sprouted out before snaking around the girl. It honed in on his genetic material in her bowels and due to the looseness of her sphincter worked itself into the orifice with no resistance. Jacob felt like he was sliding his cock back into the warm sheath of flesh.

"Now relax," she said again and the tentacle surged in circumference. A reverberating moan sounded and the woman went limp in her coils. It surprised Jacob that Shanda did moan. "Ah yes, such a human with sensitivity. I am delighted to have selected you as my catalyst."

"Please," the girl begged.

To gain more traction in assimilation, she had to persuade the woman to agree to offer herself the pleasure. In payment, an earthly form more mutually suitable between Jacob and her would be gained.

Jacob tried his best to interpret the dream. What he gathered is that somehow he was getting a play-by-play of the entire scenario. Though as of now, he wished he wasn't experiencing all of the pleasure that he was. Somehow he knew if he was awake, his cock would be straining in his pants and probably close to causing a mess. Hopefully, that didn't happen in his sleep either.

"What is it that you want?" she asked Shanda.

"Don't stop," the woman pleaded. Suddenly she felt inquisitive about Shanda.

"You want pleasure?"

"Definitely," she said with a throaty moan. "I can deliver that," she replied. "For a price."

"Whatever you want," Shanda replied with a groan. "Never let it stop."

"Why?" the alien asked. Jacob found himself bewildered too. Shana never asked what the price was. Even as the sacrifice moaned in enjoyment to the writing

"I'm so lonely," Shana said once the alien ceased anything to give pleasure. "Only pleasure makes that go away."

Jacob understood that mentality. Food used to be to him what sex was for her. A feeling to bury the hurt and pain. Jacob felt guilty that this woman was in the clutches of the monster snake that had her.

"I will grant you infinite pleasure," she replied after a bit. Jacob didn't get any indication that the alien understood. There was a feeling of excitement though that he could.

The next physical feelings were perverse to Jacob in a way he couldn't describe. An uncomfortable pressure in his anus happened and he knew then more tentacles sprang forth from the sex of the creature. He felt more pressures of pleasure as the tentacles joined in penetrating different orifices now. Nothing was safe, from the mouth, anus, and pussy, to the fact that the tentacles penetrated the ears, eyes, and even nipples. The latter being especially exquisite to him as they slid into the hard flesh. The alien woman also felt pleased with the penetration, but Shanda was definitely getting the best bargain here. The lady was shaking uncontrollably and screaming in what seemed like ecstasy. The sex may have lasted for a bit, but then the real horror for Jacob began. Jacob can't describe to himself when the change happened. He just felt as the alien's body began hardening on the outside. Sudden pulses of power heralded unknown growth. With a sudden urge, the coils loosened a bit until Shanda's head became exposed. Jaws came apart widely and the alien began the process of swallowing the girl.

There wasn't any struggle. A gag as the woman's diverse tastes hit the tongue but soon the girl and penetrating tentacles found themselves disappearing into the maw. The alien swallowed, uncoiling herself as she went down the body of Shana. The head then shoulders, which took a bit of twisting to get past, The breasts were the hardest, each round globe needing to be swallowed first. Once passed, swallowing the rest of the girl was easy. A change began happening. No longer was sight possible, a sense gone with a sudden onset of black. Then everything began feeling loose as the body dissolved away. Somewhere in it, the feeling of having a form burned away until a numbness took over. Suddenly, like a socket being plugged, Sandra was gone and all that remained was her. Her and the pleasure.

White light blinded him in his dream with it. A sensory overload that seemed to take an eternity to dissipate but when it did, he found that in the dream he suddenly discovered himself feeling suspended in the liquid.

A warm liquid that beat with the pumping of blood. He didn't feel anything else in the dream for a long time other than some pain as bones cracked and skin melted away. Whatever soup she was in, a lot was going on right now. Then Jacob got a direct address from her.

"I hunger," she spoke. He didn't know how or why, but he could feel an aching in her body. "I require more material." And then Jacob heard his name.

"Jacob," the voice said, a concerned woman's voice. The dream tore apart, and he came out of sleep.

"Wakey wakey," the girl said, and the first thing Jacob saw when he opened his eyes was glossed ruby lips. As his vision cleared, Grace came into focus.

"What's going on?" he asked blinking his drowsiness away.

"You were asleep in the library," she said with a smile and leaning down to him. He caught a whiff of her perfume, and it immediately registered not in his brain but throbbing cock how nice it smelt.

"And having good dreams."

Jacob took a moment to think. He knew she had already made a pass at him. Now that she was so close he bet whatever the alien had done to him affected her. The hand now on his leg clued him in on that too. A severe throbbing began in his cock as it strained against the fabric of his pants. Nothing in his life had prepared for a moment of wanton lust from a woman.

"A gorgeous woman will do that to you," he said before he thought about the audacity of it. Who the hell was he to say something like that to an administrator? An upper lip disappeared in succession as a tongue went across as Grace licked her lip.

"Gorgeous huh?" she said with a weird glint in her eye. "You have a lot to learn about women Jacob."

"Why don't you teach me?" he asked again without thinking. Eyes went wide with the suggestion. His own stared intently at her until her focus came back.

"I gave you my number to do just that," she said with a sudden hiss and seizing his cock in his pants. Her warm fingers around his dick made him groan in impatience. "Better yet, being that it's so late in the day, meet me out near the track field tomorrow after school and we will get to know each other."

"Why not now?" he said amused with how she responded. The surge of confidence made him feel unstoppable. He reached out to touch her leg. Much to his astonishment, she let him and he shook as his hand touched bare skin. Fingertips barely stroked the silky skin of her inner thigh, and she moaned while biting her lip. It didn't unnerve him keeping his eyes locked on green promises. With a sudden surge of bravado, he brought his hand up to touch her heat. Much to his surprise, he found his fingers in a soaked wonderland as he probed around for the unseen treasure.

"You little shit," she said with a laugh but stood straight up and removed her hand from his pants. He followed suit and pulled his hand away from her sex.

"Better keep it down," Jacob said shifting to stand up himself. "I know, and it's too late. This library is kind of small."

Somewhere else?" Jacob asked feeling a drive he hadn't before.

"It's close to the end of the day. The best I can do is write you a note for your last class," she said delivering him a now disappointed look. "There isn't enough time for us to get properly introduced."

"I agree," Jacob said allowing her off the hook. There was always tomorrow. Feeling the boldest yet, he held up his hand to her face. "Why don't you clean my fingers off?"

Grace was obviously conflicted with Jacob. The bottom lip disappeared as she bit it. Then she licked his finger, wrapping her tongue around them with a moan. Dizziness washed over Jacob as he imagined her tongue rolling across his cock like that. Cool air caressed his fingers as her warm tongue disappeared.

"I don't dare myself more," she said. "Let's get you to class."

Jacob's last class was his automotive class. When he went in with the note, everyone greeted him. The teacher even stopped teaching for the rest of the day as everyone prodded him for answers. Surprisingly to Jacob, he found he liked the attention even if he was shying away from it at many points. Thankfully no one bothered him about his hard cock either, something he hoped couldn't be readily seen by a bunch of guys.

As class concluded, Jacob left feeling an emptiness creep into him. He didn't realize that getting such positive attention or rather an interest would propel him into heights of acceptance craved since time remembered. Everyone shuffled by him in hallways eager to leave the building. Jacob meandered through the halls until he too found himself outside in the sun.

His walk didn't take him to the woods. It didn't even veer to a convenience store he frequented many times before for snacks. Instead, he walked a linear path to home.

A brisk walk didn't happen to be on the menu of the day's activities in any form before. He found that the fresh air and sun uplifted the spirit once more and the sting of abandonment faded away. With a happy gait, it took minutes to reach home instead of an hour or more.

Inside his home, Jacob again cringed at looking at how bare and ugly the entrance was. Stained carpet and bare walls told him this place welcomed few. As such, Jacob resigned to himself that with the week, the whole place would be redone. A sense of excitement went through him as hope lifted him. Maybe his father would see an improvement and praise him.

"That'd be the day," he said to himself as he walked through the house. He had pushed the door to close behind him, but then stopped suddenly when he heard it crash against the wall. Turning around he saw Billy facing him with a crazy look in his eye.

"Guess daddy isn't home huh fat boy?" Billy said walking and slamming the door behind him.

"You need to leave," Jacob said meekly, cowering as the Bully descended slowly upon him in the hall.

"Not until I punish you for earlier," the boy said.

Jacob went to say something, but with a flick of a wrist and his mind registered that the shiny object that appeared in Billy's hand was a knife. That is all Jacob needed to see before he turned and ran through the house.

"Come back here," Billy shouted, but Jacob now fit, got farther into the house and even upstairs. At the top of the stairs, Jacob froze a bit, trying to figure out where to hide. Finding nowhere, Jacob panicked and ran into his parent's room.

Jacob is almost wretched as he opened the door to go in. A smell of horror hit him and made him gag, but he pressed into the room. The humidity hit him and immediately sweetness began pouring from his body. He went by the lone window, covered by a dusty curtain, and sat against the wall there facing the door. Shaking, he wondered what to do about Billy. That is when he heard the pumping of a heart.

Looking slowly over to his left and over the bed, his parents once slept in, he looked in a horror. A sack of flesh hung on the wall. Its purple body held a yellow sac obviously filled with liquid. Jacob got the impression that it looked like a pregnant woman's swollen belly. Tendrils snaked out from the thing in black lines across the walls, ceilings, and floor. His first thought wasn't about what was going on, but how much his father would freak out with the disaster. Groaning in frustration, he was about to leave the room when Billy had rounded the corner of the hallway.

"There you are fat boy," the bully said with anger.

Jacob stood up and held up a hand as the man came down the hall. "Wait there, I'll come out."

Jacob knew himself that the words were meant to help. Billy had no idea what was in the room and neither did Jacob.

Unfortunately, though, the bully pressed on with greater speed, making Jacob realize the futility now of negotiation. Dropping his arm in defeat, Jacob waited for Billy to enter the room.

"Ready to accept your punishment," Billy said as he walked into the door frame.

Defeated, Jacob decided then whatever it took to get the scene over with he would do. Billy walked right up to Jacob anger written on his face.

"If you ever say anything stupid to me in school again," Billy said. The knife lashed out and Jacob held his arm before his mind registered that the knife had dug into the flesh of his arm. Held tight, the pain registered.

"What the hell did you do that for?" Jacob shouted at Billy. The look of surprise on Billy's face Angry himself now with the indignation of the attack, Jacob suddenly found himself attacking Billy. First, he punched the bully, a glancing blow on the arm. This turned Billy and Jacob cringed as a spray of blood hit him in the face. The knife had been pulled out. Billy got some lines of blood across his face, but that detail meant nothing as a desperate Jacob moved to hit Billy again. His second-thrown punch didn't connect. Instead, Billy had bobbed his head to the side, and Jacob put his hand into the wall. The wind went out of Jacob as Billy thrust a fist into his gut, forcing him to collapse in front of the boy.

"That's right fat boy," Billy said again. "Now I'm gonna give you a haircut."

Jacob's head was suddenly yanked back by his hair. He wheezed with tears in his eyes.

"Get ready you fat fuck," Billy said with a hiss. A hiss responded, stopping the scene. "What the fuck is that?"

Jacob felt Billy move away from him right after he let him go. Still trying to catch his breath, Jacob remained hunched over while he wheezed. Then Jacob heard the door slam closed and breathed a sigh of relief, thinking that everything was over right now. His arm hurt as his breath returned.

"Jacob, what the fuck is this?"

His attention returning, Jacob looked over to see Bill held in the air by some of the tendrils.

"I don't know," he said, which was the truth. "Get me down," the bully demanded.

Jacob stood up and another hiss was his only warning before he was entrapped too by the rubbery feeling tentacles. He didn't find himself suspended, however, instead dragged to the sac. A ripping sound tore into the room, but he barely heard it as the pumping sound became much louder as the sac become closer. Before he knew it, the cool air was across his ass. Then pleasure radiated around his dick, which quickly grew to length before plunging into the yellow sac.

If Jacob hadn't been already overcome by the pleasure, he probably would have been disgusted as his cock rubbed against the rubbery sac. Everything was warm and his cock felt like it once again had sunk into heaven.

"Master," a female voice spoke. "Yes?"

"I am glad you have finally visited me," she spoke, her words dripping with moans. "I've needed you." "What's going on?" he asked. A pulsing began around his cock, mimicking the pulses of the heart-beat-sounding nose. He went limp as he swam in the pleasure.

"I am evolving," she said. "But I needed more of your seed to continue. Why didn't you come to me sooner?"

"I was afraid," he replied. "This thing you are in hisses."

He groaned as sudden white light overtook him. It didn't register with him that he had orgasmed and subsequently passed out. The room he found himself in once again put him in front of the golden throne. Only this time, she was there.

"Is this better?" she asked. He studied her features and saw that they had changed drastically.

Is this how you see yourself?" Jacob asked.

"I can't see myself, Jacob. You are what I perceive of myself," she replied shifting around. There were a lot fewer tentacles now. Mostly it looked like they had taken up to be her hair. Her face looked human, though a bit young. She had curves too, a testament to being a follower of the unknown fertility goddess.

Naked now as she was, she didn't look to be pliable as before.

"You have a frame now," he said.

"Yes," she replied. "The woman you chose for me was more than adequate as a catalyst for myself."

"She was good?" Jacob asked, genuinely surprised by the praise.

"Her bone structure sufficed but her body's sensitivity will make worship wonderful," she said with a moan. His eyes locked onto her bountiful chest as soon as she moved to where the darker flesh of her nipples showed. "The only issues I have now center on needing more of your genetic material to finish the change."

"Why?" he asked, trying to stay engaged while drinking in the view.

"Well, everything has to be bonded. For this body to stay together and useful to me, I need your material to help me bond on the molecular level. That is until all of this body is me. Plus, without a continual supply of your seed, I can't stay on this plane."

It made sense.

"So how do I give you my seed?" he asked.

"Why you come up to this throne and fuck me," she said with a giggle.

That excited Jacob and his cock throbbed in impatience. Yet he hesitated. "What are you going to do with the other boy?" he asked.

I have to consume him," she replied with a disinterested tone.

"I find his intrusion annoying and as such he is a good sacrifice to offer up to our goddess."

"Will it be painful?" Jacob asked, unsure about the prospect of killing his tormentor. In retrospect of the question being asked he surmised that the wrong question had been asked. "Of course not," she said. "A sacrifice should be welcomed into the folds of our goddess in the way that pleases her the most; pleasure."

An epiphany hit Jacob then.

"If you kill him, we will have to explain it," he said to her. Her body shifted a bit before she got up from the throne. He watched her, mesmerized by her sexuality as her hips swayed while walking down the stairs leading up to the golden seat. Her tendril flowed, and he noticed that her hips had some and so did the v of her navel. She walked to him and grasped his cock before leaning up to his face. Frozen, he held his breath for the next words to be spoken.

"No, we won't," she said. "We, I, are beings of sex and as such, everything is to me will serve our goddess. Even now, I am draining that tormentor of everything."

"Oh," Jacob sighed, not at the statement bit because she had begun playing with his cock in earnest.

"I can't wait till we can do this in person," she said. The words weren't heard. Pleasure overrode everything and Jacob soon spasmed in a release. There wasn't anything in the dream, though. No liquid and it was something that Jacob realized.

I bet it will feel amazing," he said with a whisper. "How long will you be?" No answer.

Jacob opened his eyes and found himself looking at the yellow sac of the alien pod. The pumping of the heartbeat resounding in his ears sounded like an endless drum being pounded relentlessly. Pulling back, he found himself now disconnected from the thing. His front was covered in sticky slime. Disgusted, he took a step back. A groan made him turn around and gasp in horror.

Billy looked horrible. Everything about him sang that death approached. His skin hung on his bone, but there was no sustenance in his frame. Muscles were gone, and his head leaned back with his mouth agape. A sucking sound could be heard and Jacob realized now that Billy only wore his shirt now. His pants had fallen to the floor, his body's mass no longer able to support anything. The tentacles, of course, held the body up. He cringed seeing the body being sucked out. Shaking in disgust, Jacob left the room and Billy to the fate of being a sacrifice.

There was no longer any reason to stay there. The hot water washed down up him as he washed off the filth. Even after scrubbing, he felt dirty. Nothing lifted the growing sense of guilt that he had. Everything now had changed. It wasn't a dream. It wasn't a fantasy. The alien was coming, and it had fed now on two people. Two people, he had essentially offered up to as a way to get not only a purpose but also a promise of acceptance.

After dry heaving, Jacob worked to keep himself from collapsing into the tub of the shower. Eventually, he would make it back to his room and sit in his chair. Lost on what to do, Jacob did the only thing he could. He went back to the room.

Billy no longer hung suspended in the room. Jacob couldn't even see the boy at all when he first walked in. It wasn't until he walked into the room and could see over the right side of the bed did he see the skeletal remains of the bully. He almost hurled looking at the husk of skin that looked tightly stretched across the bones. "I'm sorry," he said. There was a shifting and Jacob turned to the pod secured to the wall. The bulbous yellow sac still looked to be similar to the pregnant belly of a woman. Shuddering in disgust, he walked up to it and put a hand on the sac. The pulsing was still there and the flesh felt warm. He noticed that the tentacles appeared to be gone now from the wall.

The only tendril snaked out from the pod and Jacob understood they helped anchor the thing to the wall. He wondered when she would emerge, the alien monster in the sack. Was it all for not? Apprehensive, Jacob sulked off to his room to pass out in his bed. His last thought about what tomorrow holds for him.

Jacob woke up again for the third time in the night. Breathing heavily as sweat poured off of him, he tried to calm down. The nightmares of swirling darkness tormented him now without abating in its cryptic message. Sitting up, he looked over at the clock.

"Damn," he said out loud to himself at seeing the clock only read a little after four in red letters. Getting up, he moved to the bathroom to relieve the pressure he had. After that, he lay back in bed and thought about his previous day.

Billy, his biggest bully, had been consumed by the apparition taking form in his parent's room. After attacking Jacob, the otherworldly being came to the rescue and Billy had been completely drained of his insides. The husk still lay next to the bed on the floor in his parent's room. Thinking about that, Jacob realized his father would be due back any day now. A new sort of fear washed over him and he began to cry a bit.

Jacob's father would not understand what was going on. Even when the man returned, what would he say or even do about his missing lover? That thought made Jacob shudder in pain. He knew the fisted blows surely to come over it. His father would know, he always knew when Jacob had done something. Two people were dead and so far the only things Jacob had gotten positive out of the experience were a promise from an alien lifeform of untold pleasures and the chance to get laid by Ms. Grace.

Ms. Grace who had made advances on him twice earlier in the day. Once in the office and another in the library. Each time Jacob had wanted nothing more than allow her what she wanted. But he had to wait all day tomorrow to get to her. Tomorrow at the track field. He made the mental note and felt better with that.

"Better to have something positive going than to keep dwelling on the two deaths," he surmised to himself. With a sigh, he decided to get up for the day. Early as it was, he bet he could accomplish a few things before he left for school.

The first thing was to search almost the entirety of the house. He avoided his father's room and his shared parent's room, but he looked for things that needed fixing. He got a list going. The first thing was replacing his father's recliner. Broken when he and Shanda fucked on the thing. The chair had been old, and it wouldn't matter what Jacob said. The fists would do all the talking in that conversation. With a shudder, Jacob found a recliner online that looked as close to the old as possible and ordered it.

Jacob quickly found as he ordered things online that he had much more money than he anticipated. Saved up over the years by his father's generous allowances and subsequently invested, Jacob ordered almost a new household worth of goods. His morning alarm going off brought him out of the trance of shopping. Blinking in surprise at the sudden intrusion, he got up and turned the alarm off.

Rubbing his eyes and stretching, Jacob felt good about what he accomplished. Granted a lot of mail would be delivered over the next few days, but with his new skinny body, he felt up to the task. Besides, if he could get most of the house finished and looking good, he bet his father would be impressed. Maybe even not notice the chair being different. Plus, something about the whole thing told him the house needed to look better anyway.

Moving from his room, he showered and completed his morning rituals. As he was getting dressed, he noticed suddenly how hard his dick had become. It throbbed hard and a thought crossed his mind. With a sigh of mock annoyance, he left, dressed, and moved to his parent's old room.

Even as he approached to open the door, he heard the pulsing of a heartbeat in liquid.

He gripped the warm know, something he knew once turned to open the door, would herald a gust of humid air. He didn't understand it, but the alien pod in the room seemed up the moisture in the air considerably. It promised queer things that Jacob did not understand.

The knob turned and he almost choked with the smell. A salty tang of heat touched his tongue and it tasted sweet. He gagged on it and quickly turned back. Having felt as if he intruded, Jacob frowned knowing his cock would have to wait now for satisfaction. Worship was the only way to whatever goddess he know pledged himself to, but self-worship seemed inappropriate to him. Never one to actually masturbate, he returned to his room and finished getting dressed.

After some breakfast, which still consisted of a few pieces of fruit and some boiled eggs, he suddenly remembered that he had Ms. Grace's number. In the previous night's festivities, he had forgotten to text her. Rushing to find his phone, he sent a text.

"Hey, it's me, Jacob."

Jacob had an iPhone. One that allowed him to see if the message had been delivered and read by the recipient. He watched in morbid fascination as not only did it swap immediately from delivered to read, but also appeared with the typing ellipses.

"Finally. Thought you forgot about me."

His stomach sank. He had never texted a girl before let alone dreamed of one responding quickly to him. It made him feel like she was excited to hear from him. Sitting there for a moment at his table, he responded.

"Had something come up and had to take care of it."

She sent back a frowny face.

"I practically waited up all night," she responded. That guilted him a bit.

"Sorry, life," he replied trying to play it off.

"Don't you want this?"

Jacob was about to reply asking what she was talking about when a picture suddenly appeared on the phone. He dropped his phone out of surprise and quickly recovered himself before picking the phone back up. A girl, no a woman had sent him a picture of her naughty parts. Parts he got to touch yesterday.

Hers was completely bare. Plump and pale with butterflied lips that glistened with moisture. Pink petals looked inviting as hell and he licked his lips thinking about how hot her pussy felt in his hands. Shaking, he responded.

"How can I not?"

"It's all yours," she replied.

"Do I still have to wait?" He asked.

The ellipses for response were typed for a long time. So much so that Jacob became aware of the time. He swore to himself before finishing dressing. Moving quickly, he gathered his school stuff and phone before moving through the house.

As Jacob left home and walked to school, he found himself disappointed that Grace didn't respond. Even as he walked into school, the phone didn't go off. He silenced the device with a heavy sigh and headed to his first class.

The class didn't mean anything to Jacob. Even as people complimented his new look and inquired about it his only thoughts centered around Grace and her gorgeous pussy. Plus, he worried constantly about her never responding. By lunch, he had lost his patience.

Walking down the halls, he went on the hunt for Grace. His first stop took him to the office where after some inquiry he learned she hadn't even shown up to school. That set him on a course of sending another text.

Jacob had leaned up against a set of lockers while he stared at his phone. He hesitated to open the thread for fear of the picture being still visible. And his nerves began setting in as he thought about what to send.

Jacob by no means felt desperate, but still, he was nervous to message again. He somehow knew that would make him seem desperate. With a shrug, he took action.

"You okay?"

The message was sent and delivered. Almost immediately it said read too. Then a reply came.

"Oh my god, I forgot to send my last text."

"Okay," he replied not knowing what to say to that. His stomach sank a bit with the realization that she had forgotten. Mostly because he didn't know what it meant.

"Seriously, can you meet me at the meeting place like right now?"

That was a question Jacob did not expect. He sat against the wall thinking of the consequences for a moment. Then another message arrived.

I literally cannot wait anymore. I'll be there in ten.

The message made him suddenly panic. How was he going to get through the school not only that fast but the break between classes had almost concluded? Swiftly he moved off the wall and navigated halls. He surmised that if he could just make it to the computer hall wing, he would be able to use one of the side doors there to leave. With a target in mind, Jacob left his leaning post and navigated the halls.

As he walked, Jacob almost wished he had his once ginormous frame. People bumped into him, many of them unaware now of who he was. Thankfully, there weren't any comments about this frame. That would have ruined the mood of everything. As he rounded a corner, he found himself suddenly in an empty hall. Any second now the bell would ring to signal the start of class.

Jacob moved quicker now. He knew the hall he needed to get to would be unwatched by teachers for stragglers. Then as he moved, a sudden thought of being caught by a teacher became a real possibility. To his surprise, when he rounded the next corner he ran right into what he didn't want to.

Ms. Devons let out a squeal of surprise as Jacob ran into her. He bounded and he heard her fall to the floor on her rump.

"I'm sorry Ms. Devons," Jacob stuttered out in horror. This woman was not the one he wanted to run into at the moment. When he suddenly felt a hand grip his hard cock, which had grown painfully hard growing down the leg of his pants. He had been so focused on moving through the halls, he had done his best to ignore it. Now that Ms. Devons had grasped it and elicited a gasp from the both of them, he throbbed even more painfully.

"Oh my god," Ms. Devons spoke before her hand let go. Jacob grabbed it and pulled her up.

Ms. Devons could only be described as a small petite woman. She wore glasses that always changed in style. It seemed to Jacob the few times he had studied her, that she pursued a life of shifting personas. Sometimes she was meek, other times powerful. Today she looked small to him and her blue eyes looked up at him with astonishment.

"I am so sorry," She said slowly as if trying to wrap her mind around the situation.

"It's okay, but, I'm late for class," Jacob replied knowing it was a lie, but the way his cock throbbed in anticipation of events to come, it didn't matter to him that he did.

"Get to class," she said, seeming to stare right through him.

"Thanks," he said and left her standing in the hallway.

He continued his way through the hall until he arrived at one last corner. Being careful this time, he slowed down enough to gather if anyone was near as he cleared it. Nobody in the halls, he went without hassling until he reached the door he sought.

No one tended to watch the doors. The halls of Silverton High happened to worry not about its students leaving. Most faculty offered engaging classes and the school's academic national ranking put it often high on the list of great schools.

Outside, Jacob blinked under the bright sun. The side entrance had few windows that watched it and the few that did, only one that rarely had an occupant. This entrance to the school opened directly next to the auditorium. Brick and stone flashed past him as he moved, a sense of urgency pulsing in his testicles. Jacob felt driven to get to the meeting place at all means.

Past the biggest part of the building were the fields. The Track field ran around two football fields while being framed by two baseball fields and two soccer fields. Woven in between the fields and track were different stadium settings like areas with bleachers, concession stands, and buildings. Jacob knew a lot of these areas, as he often had used many before to hide at lunches, and breaks and to avoid going home. He even knew how to get into some of the buildings as their locks hadn't been maintained in some years.

Moving between the buildings, Jacob realized that he had no idea what her vehicle looked like or where she would even park. There were other vehicles and so he leaned up against a wall, obscured by shadows.

"Are you here?" he sent to her.

The message was delivered but did not get read. He looked at his phone impatient that she would continue to keep him waiting. Didn't she know how much he needed relief?

Minutes passed and he looked from his phone to the cars all around. Nothing gave him a hint of where she was. The fact she hadn't read his message sent shivers of rising fear in him. His thoughts centered on this endeavor being a cruel joke. Then he heard the sound of footsteps. Panicking, he moved as far as he could in the shadows, hoping not to be seen at all.

"Jacob?" a small feminine whispered.

The voice could barely be heard and he almost missed it altogether.

"Grace?" he responded, his heart pounding in his chest.

There was shuffling in some dirt and then Jacob saw Grace. She moved slowly on the wall opposite him. She wore a floral patterned sundress with leather sandals. He could see her red lipstick from where he stood, shining in the light of the sun. Her blonde hair also glimmered in the rays of light. Grace looked like an angel to Jacob and his throat became dry.

'Where are you?" She whispered.

"Right here," Jacob said after clearing his throat. Nervous, he walked out of the shadows and into the light.

They stood looking at each other for a moment, her blue eyes darting about as she looked down the lanes.

"We are in a bad place to meet," she said. "I kind of hoped there would be more privacy."

She was biting her lip and shifting about on her feet in what looked to Jacob like impatience.

"We can't do much here," she said with a groan.

"Why can't we leave?" Jacob asked.

"There were people near my car. If I was seen leaving with a student," she said looking down. There was no need to finish the sentence as Jacob understood the implication.

"I know a place close by," he said.

She stopped moving.

"What do you mean?"

"These old buildings aren't all secured well," he replied whilst turning suddenly and walking briskly on a route to a building he knew he could break into. "Follow me."

Jacob never felt so alive in his life. The exhilaration of talking to a girl and actually having her follow him made him happier than anything in his life.

The building that Jacob chose was almost in the center of the fields. He had no idea what the building had been intended to originally be used for, but he knew that inside it had a few amenities that would be perfect for the two of them. Walking up to the door, he moved the lock and yanked hard on the doorknob. Like magic, the door popped open.

"See?" he said to Grace.

"If we didn't need this room so bad, I would have to reprimand you for this," she said. She was back to dancing on her tiptoes. "Can we go in?"

"After you," he replied.

Grace didn't wait and she went inside. He followed.

"It's a little dark," she commented. Jacob always knew the place would be.

The building had no windows and only single lights in the center of the rooms. Upgrades had never been done here and one would have to wander blindly to the center of the room to find the cord to pull. Jacob did this and soon bathed both of them in yellow light.

"This is old," she said with a circle examining the room. "At least there are things to be used."

Jacob was about to say something but thought better of it. The dryness in his throat had come back and he feared souring her mood. She stopped turning to face him.

"I would never have known this was on campus," she said. "How did you find this?"

"Hiding," he replied feeling sudden heat rising in him as his fists clenched. His gaze fell to the floor and he blinked back tears as he felt ashamed for being such a weak person.

"It wasn't right how you were treated," Grace said and her feet appeared into his view. Looking up, he was thrown back as Grace threw herself on him and wrapped herself around him. A tongue was thrust into his mouth.

He tasted the sweet cherry on her lips, its sweetness a surprise. The warmth of her tongue was too. Her kiss was sloppy but he minded not. It's as a disappointment when she broke the kiss.

"I'm gonna make it up to you as much as I can though," She said with a sudden fierceness in her voice.

Jacob didn't know what brought them to where they were within a few seconds, but he soon found himself pressed up against a wall. Hands were ripping his pants open and soon they were about his ankles. Hands rubbed his clothed crotch as she bit insistently at his ear.

"Fuck'n Christ Jacob," she said.

"What?" he replied in a panic.

"If the ladies knew you had this, let us just say you would have been much more popular."

"Thanks," he said. "You know, you're pretty yourself."

"So is your cock too I bet."

She knelt in front of him and she yanked his boxers down. His cock relished the freedom as it flopped heavily out into the air.

I have to taste it," she groaned.

Jacob wasn't sure what he expected. Maybe a lick or even kiss. But when he watched her begin swallowing his cock, all he could do is fall back against the wall and allow the sensations of the blow job to wash over him.

Sucking sounds filled the room as well as wet ones. His cock felt heavenly as she sucked on the tip. Then she was slowly jacking him off whilst looking up at him.

"I want to suck this down my throat, but I think you're too big."

Jacob could care less about it. His dick needed more stimulation now. Something washed over and he felt a surge of power inside himself.

"That's okay, you can try again after you shove it up your pussy."

The look of surprise on her face was something he relished at that moment.

"I had forgotten that I wanted to fuck," she said. "This cock is just so amazing looking."

"It's all yours right now," Jacob said with a sigh of impatience. The throbs for release become insistent.

"Seems like our friend here is getting impatient," She noted before standing up.

"I don't want you to fuck me right at this moment. That thing is too big for you to shove into me right away."

Jacob was almost insulted, but then his brain clicked to tell him she hadn't cut at him. Instead, she had told him she needed to be the one to put his cock into her. Maybe his dick had become too big, but if she wanted to ride it, there didn't need to be a complaint from him.

'There's a spot I can lay down," he said.

Grace leaned forward and kissed him once more, rubbing herself against his body. His cock sandwiched between the two of them as she did. The stimulation made him shake and by the time she broke the kiss he was panting.

"Let's go, I really can't wait any longer," she said.

Jacob kicked his pants away and moved to a set of stairs.

"There is an unused cot upstairs," he said, before going up.

He made it to the top and fumbled once more with the light. Once on, he saw at once that grace stood at the top of the stair naked.

"Sundresses are easy off and to put back on," she said.

Grace was much more petite than he realized. Her clothing the other day accentuated her chest, which sported large spheres of breasts. Big and perky, with nipples jutting out proudly. Her waist was toned and her hips a bit wider than he would have thought. Grace was gorgeous with her blond hair and red lips.

"You can pick your jaw up," she said with a giggle. "I have never stood naked before in front of a student."

Jacob wondered briefly if she had been with many students or if he was the first.

"I would never do this, only tease, but there something about you," she continued. Something told him she was feeling guilty all of a sudden and out of place.

"We don't have to," he offered. "But you won't get a chance at this cock again."

To iterate his point, Jacob went over to the cot. Surprisingly there wasn't a build-up of dust on the thing. He has down and began slowly jacking himself.

"Sure be nice to have something promised on it,' Jacob said. It was weird to him how easily he could swap from a meek person into a sexual being. Plus, it felt right too and that unnerved him a bit. What would he become when all was said and done?

Goops of pre-cum came out the tip, to which Jacob used to lather up his cock. This action lubed him up and soon he groaned in pleasure with the sensations. He closed his eyes trying to remember what sex felt like.

"Dammit," Grace said with a stamp of her feet. "I can't stand it anymore."

Jacob heard her and he opened his eyes to see Grace coming over to him. Her breasts barely moved as she walked, but her hips swung sultrily. As she walked up, Jacob didn't even bother to stop himself.

Grace wasted no time in walking up to him. Jacob soon found himself pushed onto his back and Grace's tongue back in his mouth. This time, Grace openly moaned into him and Jacob got braver in his hands.

Her breasts were firm and heavy in his hands as he squeezed them gently. A feat that was new to him, but he figured if he made her moan, that was what he should continue doing. Soon enough, his hands roamed to her nipples, to which he delightfully found she groaned throatily and shoved her tongue deeper down his throat.

"Touch me," she said after breaking the kiss. The sudden ability to breathe easier had Jacob gasping for air. "Just like you did in the library."

Reaching between them, Jacob snaked a hand down her body until he could move a finger through soaking swollen lips. He remembered that she had thick labia and they felt spongy to his touch as he rubbed over their slippery surfaces. Unfortunately, Jacob was too embarrassed to tell Grace of his inexperience with sex. Press as he may, he had no practice in female anatomy in any significant way, but he did know some things.

For how if you rubbed a hand on the firm nub hidden between the folds of a woman's labia, it would cause a great amount of pleasure to her. Jacob fumbled through slippery folds of sex until he found her clit. Rubbing vigorously on it made him jump.

"You found the right spot," she groaned.

Jacob really didn't care what she had to say about it. He found himself fascinated by finding the pleasure point. And hers seemed to be extremely sensitive.

"Oh yes," she exclaimed.

Jacob had begun rubbing vigorously on the nub. Before he knew it, he felt his hand become covered in an unknown liquid.

"You made me squirt," she cried out.

Her thighs powerfully clamped around his hand, trapping him in a painful vice. Jacob felt unprepared as she convulsed uncontrollably. The pattering of fluid hitting the floor could barely be heard through her gasps.

"Are you okay?" Jacob asked, not understanding what had just occurred. Grace had fallen silent for the most part, but her body hadn't relaxed yet. "Hey."

Grace opened her eyes and bit her lip.

'That was delicious," she said. "I needed that.

She relaxed and Jacob withdrew his hand. He tried to lean up only to be stopped when she grabbed his shoulders and shoved him back down onto the cot.

"But as it goes, you can't get too much of a good thing," she said. A fierceness in her hands told Jacob he was in some sort of trouble right at this moment. She moved and ended up straddling him around his waist. "I'm gonna be sore after this."

Jacob didn't know what else to do, but her bountiful breasts did hang in front of his face.

Reaching up with both hands, he managed to position one to suckle on.

Grace let out a throaty moan, even leaning to lower her chest for easier access to him.

He felt elated right now as his cock throbbed. The flesh of her nipple was something new to him. Heck, the whole experience was new for the most part. His first sexual encounter was way more animalistic than what currently transpired, and he lacked the opportunity to properly experience it. He didn't intend to let the second time pass.

Moving back and forth, he suckled without abandon between the two bags of flesh. He loved how firm they were, and felt strangely comforted with it. Something felt right about it and missing from his life.

"God Jacob," She cried out. He felt a warmth spread over his stomach.

"You peed on me?" he said in sudden fear as he unlatched a nipple. It was only when he did that he saw she was in another fit of convulsions. Her face contorted in what seemed like pain. As she seemed to recover, that is when she moved.

"I need your cock in me right now," she yelled. Suddenly, she moved and he found the head of his dick bouncing around looking for a comforting place to be.

He groaned in disappointment when his chest left his immediate reach as she leaned up. Watching as she reached back, he noted how flexible she appeared to be.

"One day you may get to see how flexible I am," she replied. "But today, I am just content in draining everything out of your cock that it has to offer me."

And like that, he slid up her oily cunt.

"Helps a lot that I slobbered this thing down my throat," she groaned.

"I don't know what you mean," Jacob replied, trying to keep his mind lucid as a tight hole took him in. It felt like a band of rubber being stretched around his cock as it went down the length.

"The lube my spit provides," she told him. "Let's you slide right in easily."

He could agree with that sentiment. When she sank his entire length the both of them froze not making a sound at all. Jacob could feel her heartbeat around his dick. A pulsing as her pussy squeezed repeatedly and pleasantly.

"Hey," she said. He looked from her chest up to her face. "I hope you're ready, cause I'm gonna milk your cock with my fuckhole."

Then she leaned forward and began riding his cock.

They both gasped at the machinations of her body. She rode his cock slowly, doing things Jacob wished he had a camera for. One thing was for sure, he had moved his hands to her hips to find that she had a wonderful amount of cushion there. Fingers dug into the flesh as she shifted her hips up and down.

"I'm gonna tire out with your length," she said with a moan. "But I can't stop riding it."

"Please don't," he begged her. Sex with a woman seemed to be much more enjoyable to him when she took it from him. Made him feel like she wanted him even more than presenting herself as Shanda did. A pang of guilt washed over him for a second until he remembered that Grace was just like Shanda.

A slut who needed sex to survive. Who wanted the pleasure to never end? What more was there to her life?

"I don't aim to stop boy until your balls are shriveled up raisins," she hissed while increasing her pace. "I love sex, but hot cum splashing against my womb sets me off even more."

"That's good because you keep it up," he grunted trying to concentrate on holding back the inevitable torrent of cum he no doubt would unleash into her. "I'm gonna cum."

"Don't hold back," she said. "I need it."

Her pace picked up even more, impossible as it seemed to Jacob. He heard the slick noises of their sexes being together. It was all too much for him.

"Argh," he yelled.

"Yes," she screamed in reply. "Fill my fuckhole."

Each spurt of cum came more powerful than the one before it. Powerful throbs that made grunt with their passing. He could feel his balls emptying.

"God yes," she cried out.

"Ow," he was his reply. Her long nails scratched down his chest leaving a feeling of fire in the paths. Still, he continued to cum. A fire hose that refused to cease in its dousing mission. After his orgasmic release, Jacob relaxed with a warm feeling washing over his body.

"That was incredible," she said getting off of him. She fell on the cot next to him. Things were bigger than he expected, but then as curvy as she was, she wasn't big. "I want you to take a picture of your cum leaking out, then we can go back to fucking."

"Okay," Jacob replied getting up from the cot. He found a phone thrust into his hand.

"Kneel and take as many pictures you can as I push out your cum," she said. "There is a lot of it."

Grace had lain down and he watched as her chest heaved.

"Go there is so much," she said between heavy breaths.

Jacob didn't reply. Instead, he knelt down between her legs. He pulled the camera app up on her phone.

"You don't keep your phone locked?" He asked snapping a few pictures of her angry red lips The petals of her pussy inflamed in an even angrier red. Her clit had become swollen and engorged fully or so it seemed to him. It could have been hiding before when he fingered her as he did not expect to see the dime-sized dome of glistening flesh poking out so proudly out of her meat curtains.

"No need to," she said. "Concerning the situation, I love to take pictures of my creamy cunt or myself often. Need two phones with my career field."

Jacob thought for a moment and worried that she had many pictures of her cunt full of cum.

"You ready?" she asked.

"One sec," Jacob replied. He set up the phone and snapped a few photos of her pussy. "Ready."

I'm gonna spread myself first," she told him.

Jacob didn't respond but took pictures of her pussy as she moved fingers to spread her outer labia. As they spread, she groaned.

"It's still so hot."

A few seconds elapsed and then the white creamy goo began flowing through her meaty lips. He marveled with each press of the photo-taking button at how astonishingly gorgeous a woman's sex was. Her hidden hole blinked open and shut many times and then, began sputtering the thick goo out.

"Oh god," she cried out. "It's going down my ass."

Sure enough, the cum was doing that. Viscously flowing out of her gaping hole. Jacob marveled at his handwork creamily flowing down to and across the bud of her ass. Even though he snapped pictures continuously, the sight of pink butthole being covered slowly in cum made his cock spring almost painfully back into the ready position. Then another sight about it made his mind reel in memory.

Shanda's puckering asshole became called to mind. Ridged fissures of her sphincter that anus were not as pronounced as Grace's but he knew the woman had enjoyed anal sex extensively. Grace's asshole looked well used to Jacob as the ring of her anus happened to be swollen and way bigger than the dime-sized of Shanda's. This anus happened to be the size of a half dollar and the fissure from its edge was thick and canyon-like as they traveled into dark depths. Feeling bold and without warning, he rubbed the white cum around it.

"Oh, you tease," Grace groaned. He applied more pressure against its elastic tissue. She began breathing heavier once more.

It's warm," Jacob commented.

"You're gonna find out shortly how much warmer if you keep doing that."

"Oh, I don't need the threat," Jacob said looking up and locking eyes with her. His finger sunk intc the orifice with no resistance.

"God, you're bold."

"Says the office slut on the cot with a student,' he replied. A second finger joined the first.

"You're being mean," she said with a moan.

"Would a cock be better?" he asked.

Jacob didn't wait for a reply. He put the phone gently on the floor and moved up between her legs. Her eyes didn't move from his as he sunk his cock back into her cunt.

"What are you doing?"

"Lubing my cock up for that ass," he replied. She bit her lip.

"I don't know what it is, but the surprises keep coming."

"What do you mean?" Jacob replied taking his cock out. Her mouth opened up as if to say something. He looked down and positioned his cock against her puckering anus. The fissures of her ass rubbed pleasantly against the head of his dick.

'You just seem so shy and quiet," she replied.

"Is that what you like?" Jacob asked rhetorically. "Finding a young man who is shy so you can destroy their innocence?"

Jacob had begun raising his voice, but he had a smile on his face.

"Don't be mean," she cried out. He didn't know if that was because of what he said or due to the head of his cock pressing up against his eager sphincter.

"Mean," Jacob said with a laugh. "Mean would be taking this cock away wouldn't it?"

Grace let out a gasp, horror written all over her face.

"Please just stick it up my ass," she begged. "I can't live without you up my ass."

"Without me?" Jacob said out loud. No one had ever said something so remotely as needing him in any way. In fact, Jacob had felt earlier when asking about her desire for a young inexperienced male that it could have been any. The insistence that he needed "Him" was something of a surprising conundrum for Jacob. This slut wasn't just one who wanted cock, she needed his cock. Up her ass. What woman used those coupling of words for anyone?

"Yes, god yes just fuck me," she cried out in a desperate plea. He almost freaked out when he locked eyes with her and saw her eye shadow running in black down her cheeks. With an intake of air, he obliged her desperation and sank himself into her bowels.

The heat once again hugged his cock and the sensation was softer to plow his dick against. It felt different to from his first experience, and Jacob felt more in control having his cock where it was. Even as he pulled his cock out of the sheathing orifice, Grace had fallen quiet.

"You okay?" he asked, feeling genuine concern, but in reality, he couldn't stop himself from what he was doing. At this moment, she was something to be used right now for his enjoyment. As he moved, he looked at her and had a bad realization.

Grace's eyes were rolled into the back of her head. While the sounds of his cock clicking in and out of her ass dominated the noises, he relaxed seeing that she still breathed. He stopped though.

"Hey," Jacob said. There was no reply from her. Her eyes were closed now. Feeling suddenly ashamed and exposed, Jacob did the only thing his mind could think up of. He stopped having sex with her.

His dick popped out and he almost freaked realizing that she passed out, she may not remember anything about their encounter. So he placed her on the cot completely and grabbed her dress, which he placed onto her form as best he could. Not knowing what else to do, he headed downstairs and dressed.

Picking his phone up off the ground, where it had fallen before, he decided to take a course of action that would placate his fear. Right now, Jacob had nothing if Grace woke up and panicked herself.

Moving back upstairs, he was assaulted by the scent of sex hanging in the air. He moved through it cautiously as if he were hiding in a fog. Moving quickly, he grabbed her phone and began sending himself everything on it he could find. Surprisingly, Jacob didn't find much in concerns about sex. Only pictures that he had taken of their encounter. There were tons of pictures of herself in various poses and outfits. All sent to himself.

Finishing, he did check on her once more. She didn't rouse at all. Feeling bad, he sent a text to her explaining the situation and to call him when she awoke. In all actuality, the whole thing left Jacob unsettled as he had never been in the situation.

'Waiting around seems like a bad idea," he said out loud to himself.

He let out a sigh of despair before deciding to leave.

Walking out of the building on the baseball fields was always a nerve-wracking event for Jacob. Being caught using the buildings by an administrator would be one thing, but if any of his bullies followed then the hideaways would end up being torture areas. Maybe now they would be fucking areas.

Opening the door slowly, he peered out before realizing that night had fallen. The sight made him check his phone and over three hours had passed since he had snuck into the building. Feeling brave now that night had fallen, Jacob left the building.

Walking through the fields Jacob found himself unmolested. No one happened to be around and he went through the fields quickly before reaching the brighter sidewalks.

Jacob's pace was slow as he walked under the streetlights. The night air was cooler than yesterday and he found himself having missed the walks to and from school. Something that he hadn't crossed his mind as he spent his last days at home.

He checked his phone often, hoping that Grace would text him at some point telling him she was okay. With no luck, he walked down streets navigating them with confidence that there wasn't lurking in wait.

A slight breeze rustled trees and Jacob began whistling. He felt great except maybe for the uncomfortableness of his cock. It was still swollen, but when he put his pants on, he had tucked the throbbing member up past the waistband. The head pushed against his belly button with its curve, but he paid it no mind as he walked. The throbbing from the lack of release bothered him, but walking dulled it.

Looking up, he saw the moon and found himself lost in its luminous brilliance. The stars complimented the night with it, sharing in the beauty. He thought it funny how he never looked at the stars before. Then again, he also never stayed out late either on account of his father.

As he walked now, he thought of the man that was his father. The man was late coming home. Business trips could last like that, but Jacob was sure that his father had probably taken a vacation on the return. Such actions had been taken before and even once when he was much younger, Jacob had been home alone for over a month. His father showed up one day, beat him as usual and life went on. No explanations, no love, and no life.

A tear fell down his face as he walked down the street to his house. The flashing lights of red and blue on the street in front of his house made him utterly panic. Taking some breaths, he went home fast.

As he walked down the sidewalk, a cop in full uniform walked up to him.

"Hold on there," the officer said quickly betraying her gender before he could tell.

"What's going on?" Jacob asked fearing that his father had come home and found the alien in the bedroom.

"There's a gas leak further down the street," she said.

It took a moment for that to register in his mind.

"Gas?"

"Yeah, a couple of houses down. The Millers had a line open up. We have everyone staying back from their place until the all clear is given."

There wasn't a find. Jacob checked the driveway. No car that matched his father's. Just a few emergency vehicles sitting with lights whirling in their different colors. With a sigh of relief, he asked how long the wait would be.

"Not much longer now. They had to dig the line-up and once it is changed out, everyone can go home."

"Okay cool."

"Where do you live?"

"Right here," Jacob replied pointing at his house.

The female cop blinked at him in surprise.

"I'm so sorry we didn't realize anyone would be home," she said to him.

"Don't worry about it," he said. "Just want to go in."

"You actually can," she said. "You're outside of the zone."

"Good," Jacob said before moving on. A crazy thing for him was that she was an authority figure. Normally he would have been too terrified to do such things. "Have a good night officer."

If she responded Jacob didn't hear. He walked up briskly to his door and quickly let himself inside. Securing the door, he moved to check the entirety of the house for security. Something that should have been done before. The front door may have been locked, but if anyone came inside the house through the unlocked back door or windows, they could find out.

The chore done, Jacob's stomach growled. Moving to the kitchen, he fixed a healthy dinner, stripping his clothes while he did. After eating, he headed upstairs to shower.

After the shower, Jacob knew there was one thing left to do. He needed to check on the lifeform in his parent's bedroom. That worried him as he had no idea what would be in store for him when he did. It took him ten whole minutes to work up the nerve to check. Mostly because of the flashing lights that rebounded through window curtains. If the lifeform had a plan of action or anything went wrong, cops were nearby to intervene. Moving to the room, Jacob opened the door slowly. A humid heat of hair did assault him like it did that morning accompanied now by a salty pleasant scent. The second is that the cocoon that held the alien priestess had drastically changed.

The pod on the wall that looked like a pregnant belly did not look like it was pregnant anymore. A hole in the yellow membrane had spilled the liquid contents onto the floor, which had stained the carpet green and yellow. That stain radiated out and covered almost the entirety of the carpet in the room.

Something moved inside the pod. A slushing of sorts and more liquid spilled to the floor. Tendrils had drooped from their anchors and the pod now looked sickly to him. There wasn't life contained within its cells anymore.

Another slushing sound came from the emptying sac. Nervous, Jacob did the one thing that his instincts screamed not to do. He made a noise.

"Hello?" he said. The moving that had been going on stopped.

A weird breathing noise could be heard resounding from the sac.

"Do you need help?" he asked not even knowing why he did. The pounding in his ears told him to run. But he couldn't move.

"Jacob," it spoke his name with a hiss. More weird breathing noises. "I can smell that it's you."

"It is," he said.

"I'll release you then," it said once more in a raspy voice.

Then it felt like a weight had been suddenly lifted off of him.

"You are about to see my glorious birth," it said. How fortuitous for you."

"Uh thanks," Jacob responded honestly not wanting to be in the room any longer. It may be here because of him, but he didn't know what was about to exit the opening pod.

"It's my thanks," it said in its raspy voice. "It's taking me a bit to set my new body up."

"Is that why your voice is raspy?" He asked the question before he thought about it being rude to the alien.

It laughed in response.

"Sorry," he said looking down as heat burned into his cheeks.

"Don't be, I need the feedback," it said.

Moments passed. Jacob sighed and moved to lean against the wall. From there he spied the dried-out remains of Billy laying still in the same position from his death. That sight made Jacob shudder in guilt feeling that the poor guy didn't truly deserve the way he died.

"Jacob," a heavenly feminine voice said. "I think I have the voice correct now."

I'll say," he said, genuinely surprised with the change.

"It sounds good?"

"Like heaven spoke itself," he said with a smile.

"That's supposed to be a compliment," she said, and then there was a second of silence. "Yes, it was. Thank you."

"There will be many more I think," he said.

"As long as it's all for the betterment of worship."

She was referring to sex. Jacob knew that.

"I worshipped with a woman earlier," he said.

"I know, that was meant to be," she said. "She is changing as we speak." "What do you mean?"

Sloshing in the pod was his response. He watched as the taunt grey-looking skin of the belly moved around. Something wriggled underneath and even though Jacob had no idea what it would look like, it didn't worry him that a monster may emerge from the pod. He figured this situation was either great, to which it had been for the most part. Or the situation would dissolve into a poor one and then, he figured there would be no need to worry.

Sighing, Jacob turned over to look at the bed his parents once used more than a few years ago. He worried that his father would see that someone had been in the room. Besides the fact that the pod was present and so was a body.

"You worry too much," she said. At least, he hoped it was a she. That was the whole point of offering a female up to her to bond too is so that she would be. Gender seemed to be a fluid concept to her kind, or rather whatever she was.

"I try not to," he said sheepishly. "Are you okay?"

"Of course," she replied. "I am currently just disseminating memories and figuring out this body that I have."

"Oh," he replied.

"It's different. While the woman grew up with this, this is my first time possessing a physical form."

Jacob found that understandable.

"We have a huge mess to clean up," he said after a moment.

"Don't worry about the body or this pod. Both are easily disposed of."

As if to support the statement, a tentacle fell from the ceiling to the floor and landed with a crunch. In moments it began cracking before disintegrating into dust.

"What about you?"

"I am not so easily disposed of, but I will require a bath and food soon."

"I can handle both," he said. "Be back soon."

Jacob tore out of the room. It may have been getting late into the night, but Jacob rushed out of the house excitedly. There weren't many reasons not to.

The first thing was to get would be things for a woman to bathe in. Running as fast as he could, something that didn't even register to him that he was doing, he went down lighted streets until he reached a department store.

Shopping for someone other than himself was entirely new, especially before when Jacob's weight prevented him from shopping in the store himself. He always shopped online. The experience was lost on him as he stood in the aisle of body soaps. He had no idea what to really get, so he grabbed three different liquid body washes. Then he was off to do the same for shampoos and conditioners. He matched flavors and then moved to find toothpaste and vaginal washes.

After a few moments, he realized he needed a cart and went to the front to get one. No one bothered him as he went back to buy deodorants and perfumes. He even grabbed a few different lubes. Everything he gathered wasn't just for her either, he realized quickly that anything that would aid in 'Worshiping' on her side of things, then he needed to provide it.

Also moving quickly, he got some clothing items for her. Being that money wasn't a big deal to him, he bought a few different sizes of clothing that didn't have numbers but letters of sizes. He assumed and hoped that she would fit between small and large sizes. After getting sweat pants, shorts, underwear, and a few shirts he went over to the men's side and bought a few shirts to fit himself. Not wanting to offend if by chance what he bought she didn't like. Thinking about that, he went back and bought a few sundresses too.

Food was the last thing to buy. He had no idea what to get her for that. Moving fast, he grabbed a variety of foods, including sweets. After finishing and checking out, which thankfully there were self-checkout stations, he left.

Standing outside, Jacob only now realized a major flaw in his outing. He had no way of walking with the items. No car owned or even a person to call for a ride. Sighing, Jacob did the only things he could think of to do. Looking around and feeling altogether like a criminal, Jacob left the department store and traveled home.

Thankfully, Jacob knew he could take side roads to get home. Less traveled ones, but it would take longer to get home. So far, Jacob surmised he had been gone for over an hour. The what-ifs piled up in his mind and more than once, he stopped to keep himself from hyperventilating.

Home neared and Jacob had a full-on panic attack seeing the flashing lights in the distance. In his rush, Jacob hadn't even considered the emergency down the street from his house. A street over and he would be home. Right now, he stood on a plane in another existence trying to figure out his problem. On one hand, there was the option of leaving the cart in the backyard. A tall wooden fence hid the yard. The issue was, that meant leaving the card in the open next to a neighbor's fence. That would surely mean that if he was stopped or held up the cart wouldn't necessarily be there when he made it back. On the other hand, meant walking up to his home with the cart. With a deep breath, he chose the latter.

Walking down his street pushing a cart probably wasn't the oddest or worst transgression on his block. Jacob didn't live in the best part of town it was far from the worst. There still happened to be homeless who occasionally frequented the area. Pushing the cart, Jacob moved closer to home and the emergency vehicles.

The cart moved especially noisier as he approached home. He never realized how covered in loose gravel the sidewalks had. As he approached home the same blonde cop from earlier approached him.

"Hey you need to stay back," she said to him. "Oh, it's you."

"Yeah, it's me," he replied feeling sheepish and scratching his head.

'You rushed out so fast earlier," she said.

"Yeah was in a rush. Had to run an errand for my dad and well," Jacob motioned to the cart full of stuff.

"You stole the cart?"

"Not on purpose, but I didn't have another way to carry my stuff," he said. He saw her tense up. "I plan on returning it."

He held his hands up and put on a face of despair.

"I don't know if I can let this slide," she said biting her lip. "You have a receipt?"

"Yes," Jacob replied. He dug through his pockets and produced the slip of paper to the officer. She snatched the receipt from him.

"Let me see this."

Jacob sat there in his annoyance, but he didn't let it be known how annoyed he was. She went through every bag and checked.

"You have an interesting haul here."

"My dad is bringing home some new girl from overseas and apparently she didn't have clothing. He didn't tell me sizes."

"Oh," she replied.

"Yeah, this is really awkward for me too," Jacob said again scratching the back of his head.

"Get the cart back by tomorrow night," she told him handing the receipt over to him. He took the paper and almost cringed when their skin touched. "I'll be by to check and make sure you returned it."

She walked off her radio cackling in noise. Letting out his breath, he pushed the cart up to his front door. Opening the door, he quickly moved the bags inside and left the cart on the porch before going in.

The food was the first priority. Putting it up quickly, he moved to grab the soaps first. Moving upstairs, he worried about what sight would greet him when he entered his parent's bedroom.

Jacob wasted no time in walking in and putting the bags of soap onto the bed. He did catch that Billy no longer lay where he was. Noting that a dusty end was probably the cause, he turned to the apparatus on the wall.

There was no hint of life at all in the thing. The outside looked like tree bark and the only thing still hanging was the actual pod, which had turned white in totality.

"You there?" he asked.

"Yes," she replied. "My skin has hardened.'

"That's good," he replied having no idea what she was talking about.

"I'm ready to emerge."

She didn't even wait for him to reply. Instead, the white sac ripped open and he watched as a human woman emerged. That sight surprised the hell out of Jacob. He didn't expect her to look human or like a woman at all. She came out and he drank the view in as she stretched.

This woman was an avatar of fertility. She had an hourglass figure with a voluptuous body. He could see just from her hip size that her backside was big. His tiny waist was toned. Her breasts perked up with their grapefruit size with giant jutting nipples.

She stopped stretching and dropped her arms to her side. Black hair shined like obsidian and stretched down past her shoulder. Her eyes blinked with giant red irises and black pupils Her nose was small, her face reserved, and she looked astonishingly beautiful.

"What do you think?" she said with a smile.

"I uh," Jacob had no words. His mouth hung agape at the sight of her.

"I am here now Jacob," she said.

Jacob sat on the edge of his parent's bed trying to understand everything in his world. The pod was gone now, dissipated into dust just like Billy and the tentacles that once spread across the room. In fact, now the room looked no different than before she had shown up. And he did mean she now.

Her sex was undeniable now. A difference cemented by the full female form with the body. Her curves screamed "milf" and he had trouble understanding why she chose such a voluptuous form. Not that he found her unattractive, but it seemed to be unmatched by women his age.

Right now, she was using the shower in his parent's room. Only god knew the last time the bathroom had been used. All he knew, is that after she had asked to take one, she had freaked out over the soaps he had gotten and the clothes. The clothes sat on the bed near him, still tagged and new. He had thought to wash them but refrained from such things. The last items he bought for her from his earlier trip to the store were some hair care products, lotions, and food. The last item was downstairs.

'Jacob.

He heard his voice being called out. A melody that dripped with honeyed promises. It made his head swim as he relaxed with his name being spoken in such a way.

"Jacob."

"Yeah," he replied to her.

"I'm hungry."

"No problem," he said before getting up off the bed and leaving the bedroom.

Jacob was glad to have something to do. Sitting around and waiting in anticipation of whatever would come had been plaguing him. Plus, he had been constantly checking his phone for some sort of sign from Grace that she was okay. After leaving her earlier passed out in the building on the fields at his school, he worried the sex had done something bad to her.

Then there were the cops. The lights from the emergency vehicles outside still flashed through the windows. It reminded him now of the female cop who had stopped him twice that day trying to enter his home. The last stop had been when he had returned with a shopping cart full of the stuff for his visitor. He stopped in the hall to sigh.

"So much going on," he spoke to himself, before heading down the stairs and to the kitchen. He turned on some lights and began pulling food out to cook. Being that Jacob cooked often for himself and his father, the task itself took little to accomplish. By the time he finished and turned to set the table, she was standing there and leaning against the door frame of the kitchen.

Gah," Jacob exclaimed almost dropping the food to the floor.

"That smells good," she said before moving over to him. He noticed then that she had a more petite form now.

"You can change your form?" he asked.

"No talk, just eat."

She grabbed the plate of food from him and sat at the table. The chair creaked as she sat down, something that Jacob automatically attributed to being his fault. She had sat in the chair he often did, but he smiled knowing that within the next few days, new furniture would be here. His thoughts were interrupted suddenly by slurping noises.

Jacob had cooked a few different vegetables, a couple of steaks, and some baked potatoes for their meal. As he watched her, he saw that he wouldn't be eating anything he fixed as already most of the food looked devoured.

"Is it good?" he asked.

She mumbled some sort of reply. It was incomprehensible with the slurping and smacking sounds. For a being of sex, she sure seemed to be one of gluttony instead. That thought made him chuckle to himself.

"I'm done," she said leaning back in the chair. She let out a burp and he remembered there wasn't a drink. Turning quickly, he brought her a glass of sweet tea. She took it and drank it enthusiastically. Feeling dismissed, he walked away from her and headed back upstairs in amazement at what happened.

Granted, he registered that she had put on some clothes at least. They looked a bit big on her, but he did think she looked cute. With the black hair and freckled light skin, she seemed to have found the perfect human form.

Jacob went back to his parent's bedroom to check on everything. Much to his surprise, the room looks untouched. Even looking in the bathroom, he noticed that nothing had been left for discovery.

"I moved it all into your room," she said, making him once again jump in surprise. "You seem to worry too much."

"Jesus," he hissed turning to her.

"I know you have problems with your father," she spoke as a matter of fact. "I don't like how anxious it makes you."

"Well, I did order new furniture for the place to help out, but this room belonged to both him and my mother."

"Where is she?"

The woman, as he didn't know what else to call her, asked hard questions fast. He sat on the toilet while she leaned against the door frame of the bathroom.

"She died."

"I'm sorry to hear that," she spoke. "Based on the memories of the one I absorbed, it explains your physical and emotional state when we met."

Jacob looked at her and cocked his head in astonishment.

"I knew it was too good to be true," he sat looking away in shame.

What was?

He looked back over to her, tears stinging his eyes.

"You took that as a mean comment?"

"Well, you chose me out of pity right?"

Her eyes shot up.

"That is what I can say, an unfortunate way of looking at it. I chose you because for one, you were a loner with few ties to society and for two, I actually liked you."

Jacob got up and brushed passed her on his way by. He barely heard the queer-sounding growl before he found himself landing roughly onto the soft top of the bed. It groaned loudly in protest underweight it hadn't experienced in years. He had his eyes closed, bracing himself for the inevitable blows headed his way. When they didn't land, he opened his eyes.

"What are you doing?" She asked him while her face hovered inches above his. Her eyes, dark black eyes, locked with him.

"I heard a growl and thought you were gonna punish me," he replied not knowing why he felt so ashamed saying that.

Her head cocked.

"I do not, and I wouldn't know why. You walked by and I caught a whiff of you," She told him. "A whiff that smelled so tantalizing."

Oh.

Jacob didn't know what else to say at the moment. Other than mentioning his parent's room.

"What better way to consummate our partnership and love than on the very thing that heralded you into the world."

"I uh."

Jacob never got to finish his thought. He may have been ready to protest or even talk of his uncomfortably. As soon as her lips pressed against his, soft lips that promised future pleasures with a hot probing tongue, all of it went out the window.

He instinctively placed his hands on her hips, noting how soft they felt and almost gel-like. She moaned into him, hot tongue continually dancing in his mouth. She suddenly broke the kiss and he locked eyes with her. They were a solid magenta now and he understood then that eye color would be important.

"I've waited so long for the pleasures of the flesh," she murmured to him. Magenta shifted to a pink. A long tongue fell out of her mouth. "There is so much to experience that I don't know where to begin."

He thought it odd that she could talk without sounding like her mouth was full. The tongue pulled back in.

"Taking clothes off is a start," Jacob offered. Right now, the drive for sex had kicked in. Like a switch, there was a growing surge of confidence suddenly present.

"Clothes would be fine," she said.

She got off him and stood at the foot of the bed. He sat up and looked at her.

'You first," she told him.

'You've already seen me naked," he said to her.

"My body holds untold and inexperienced pleasures," she countered. Her eyes narrowed and she licked her lips. "And besides, I know how horny I am, I want to see that throbbing cock before letting you see how wet I am."

At the mention of throbbing, he experienced that exact sensation. He felt embarrassed but peeled his shirt off.

"So how can you tell if you actually turned on now?" He asked while undoing his pants. They pulled down leaving him in boxers and socks.

"I have the equipment now to enjoy such things.'

He didn't reply feeling altogether satisfied with the answer. Though he wanted to believe in more devout blindness. Socks joined the pile of clothes and underwear too. A look over at her, and he realized a problem.

"What is your name?"

"I don't have one. As a worshipper of our Goddess, I have never been granted one before."

"Can I name you?"

She took off her shirt, leaving her chest bared for him to look at. Her breasts were nice and round but only looked to him to be comparable to d-cups. Just over a handful, but he was no expert on the mammaries of women. The shirt dropped to the floor, and he barely got to notice that her upper torso and shoulders were freckled. Her breasts also had no nipples, but each one sported an area that looked like pursed lips.

"Why is that important right now? All you should be as focused on me stripping for you," she said as a matter of fact. "Does this form not please you?"

"No," he replied holding his arms up in defense. Her eyes narrowed at him. A dangerous-looking form of yellow appears. "I love the way you look but a name would add a level of familiarity that would make this better."

"Oh Jacob," she exhaled in excitement before moving over to him and hugging him. "I knew I chose right when I chose you."

He breathed a huge sigh of relief in his mind at saving the situation.

"So what do you want to call me?"

Jacob looked past her in a panic. A question he didn't actually expect to answer. In his sudden anxiety, he spied a picture of his mother.

"Aurora," he stuttered out, and almost immediately wished he hadn't.

"I love it," she cried out, showering him in kisses. "Keep saying it."

He repeated the name, and his hands grabbed his cock. Jerking him off made the guilt of the name dissipate a bit.

"That's right, just keep it up."

He had no idea where she was going with everything, but sat on the edge of the bed still, as she kissed his chest. Quite suddenly, his cock was buried down her throat. No warning was given, just a vacuum of suction on his entire length. The feeling was much more intense as she sucked him off.

"Oh god," he cried out, shaking as she drank down his length. Nothing in life prepared him for it. Not even the two women before had provided such sensations. It just felt right.

He looked down at her, only to find colored eyes watching him. Their eyes locked, an unspoken bond as her fuchsia bored into him. That look made him feel as if his soul had become exposed. She slurped and he tensed.

"I'm coming," he cried out and unleashed himself down her throat. The vacuum didn't let up and she closed her eyes as she drank him down. That was the sight he saw as he closed his eyes and enjoyed the intense orgasm. Still, as he tapered off, she didn't stop sucking and while he anticipated being oversensitive to the orgasm, that feeling never came.

"Are you gonna stop?" he asked worried and opened his eyes.

She slurped once or twice more before allowing his spent cock to slide out of her mouth. A smacking noise filled the air and she moaned. When her eyes opened, they were icy blue.

"That was tasty," she said after a moment. "So thick and sweet."

Jacob had always thought cum was supposed to be salty, but he didn't want to correct her. Instead, he tried to stay lucid as a wave of relaxation washed over him.

"So, for our first worship, I feel this was productive," she spoke, nodding her head in agreement with herself. It left Jacob bothered that there actually hadn't been any sex. Feeling a bit slighted, he came out of the relaxing fog.

"We aren't done," he said.

I think so for now, your tool isn't hard for the occasion.

Suck on it again," he commanded.

She cocked her head in confusion.

"Why would I want to do that, you already gave a more than adequate offering?"

"Because you haven't gotten to experience the pleasure of the flesh yet."

She stood up and stretched. He saw that the front of her shorts was wet with moisture. He knew that meant she was hornier than all hell. So why did she not want to be pleasured? Maybe she worried, but he took it as a sign he should make the move. Reaching out, he ripped her shorts down.

"What are you doing?" She cried out. There was some resistance, but Jacob managed to pull her sopping cunt against his face. A few licks and she began cooing.

Jacob found her taste phenomenal on his tongue. There wasn't time to look at what she looked like, but he could tell that by the way, her sex cushioned his face, that her sex was swollen and plump.

Ass firm in his hands, he pulled her hips forward. When the heat suddenly got cool, he barely registered that she had lifted a leg up to put on the bed next to him. That action spread her legs and drove the heat of her ass into his fingers. He thought he could barely even feel the different flesh of her anus on a few of his fingers, but his mind quickly went to the grinding against his face.

"Oh this feels good," she moaned. Jacob just continued to lap her up and hold her ass in his hands. Honey flowed out of her, and he sloppily licked up everything he could while it freely flowed out. "I need more."

The bed felt soft under his shoulders and he didn't mind the weight on his face as she straddled his head. Soon, pussy juices smeared across every inch of his face being that he could no longer drink them fast enough. He remarked to himself under her, that the other two women hadn't produced as much.

There were words being said, but he couldn't hear them. Underneath her and with all the frantic grinding, the only thing he could hear was the slippery sounds of her cunt rubbing on his face. He did try still to continue eating her out, but his tongue moved blindly through folds of pussy lips and labia. Then a rumbling sounded, faint at first, but then it grew.

Jacob had no warning but then, he surmised that neither did she. When her thighs clamped hard around him, he closed his eyes. The shaking of flesh was immense and then the spray of intense liquid almost burned his face as it hosed him down. When all was done, she fell off him and onto the bed face first.

"Wow," he commented loudly. "That was something else."

Her breaths come laboriously and heavy. He scooted out from underneath her and stood up at the edge of the bed. Turning around he noted that she had fallen in a way that presented her ass and pussy to his hungry gaze.

Everything that could have been described as female genitals was red and swollen. It even took him a back to see that strings of juice flowed slowly from the hole. Her anus looked ridged and whatnot, but didn't gape or anything. Not that it mattered to Jacob. What mattered is how sopping wet and inviting her pussy looked.

A cock, his cock, rose to meet the occasion. Announcing its willingness in powerful throbs as it grew into length. He hoped she was ready to continue their worship, but he still didn't know who or what they worshipped. Some unnamed goddess, but being that worship only meant sex in the long run, he wasn't going to complain about not knowing.

Somehow, getting up behind her and positioning himself to fuck her felt right. After all, she had presented her sex. A signal for more than ogling as he did feel the heat.

"Are you ready?" he called out to her. She moaned in response to him. Pushing his hips forward, he tried a few times to enter only to understand that he did lack experience.

"Wait," the priestess calls out suddenly. "I want to face you for my first time."

Within seconds, Jacob found himself between her legs now as she lay before him. Much to his delight, he felt more comfortable too in this position.

"You seem to have changed your idea of stopping," he said to her, locking eyes now with pink.

"I want more of this pleasure," she replied. "Now fuck me."

"You sure you want to be fucked?"

"We are worshipping, what else is there?"

Nothing at all to Jacob. He reached down and rubbed the head of his cock up and down her slit. The smooth lubed skin was hidden between the folds of her ginormous swollen labia that she sported. It sent a shudder through him, and she had gone back to huffing her horniness. With a smile, he suddenly pushed himself into what he could only feel was mind-numbing heaven.

"Oh," she cooed. He would have joined her, but without deep concentration on the task of sinking into her, he felt stopping would be as far as he made it. Eventually, their pubis met and there wasn't any way her could push himself further into her.

How does it feel to lose your virginity," he said to her.

Is that what you call sex for the first time?"

"Yeah," he said trying to keep himself from

cumming. He couldn't believe that her sex possessed such a different feeling than the other two women. It was tight, hot, and slippery for sure, but it seems to mold right to his cock, like it was specifically designed for him alone.

"Well, the woman I took the human form from happened to have a lot of sex. You chose well, as this body is sensitive beyond measure with my matriculations and changes."

"Just like me?"

"You're not inhuman like me in many ways. Granted, I may have been able to choose your sex as opposed to the female, I think in my conclusions, women on your planet wield far more power."

"How do you figure?" Jacob asked, genuinely meaning the question as a logical one rather than one of defiance to her statement. The conversation also helped him lose his focus on how sensitive his own cock had been buried in her.

"Look at you, you're helpless right now."

Jacob look down and he wished he hadn't. Where her outer labia should have been instead they weren't. They were pulled upwards like how a spider would raise its front legs in defense. He could also see small tendrils snaking out from the maw.

"What is that?"

"My sex, and if you know what's best for you, you should try to escape."

He looked up at her and saw red mixed with pink. Red always meant anger, and he figured he should. As such, he yanked his hips back in an attempt to free himself. Cock slid through her love tunnel to exit, but it stopped. He looked up at her in horror.

"Now really look at what you have sunk yourself into," she commanded.

Hesitating, he looked down. It looked like a bunch of spaghetti noodles had latched themselves to his cock. They moved, spreading themselves evenly to cover it in juices.

"I said inhuman, which also means I possess many abilities. I wanted to find out before we went on, but your eagerness is pleasing to me."

"What's gonna happen to me?" Jacob asked, completely terrified about what the red in her eyes meant.

"Sex Jacob," she replied her eyes shifting now to complete pink once more. "sex is gonna happen to you."

He didn't understand how a moment ago he was in charge of the situation and how it now, had swapped to her authority. A look of concentration came across her face and he felt a pull on his loins.

"Sex and more love than you can ever imagine," she replied. "You and I will be harbingers to this world."

Suddenly he bottomed out in her once again. He groaned with conflicting emotions.

"You've embraced me thus far, all you need to do is feel the vision I bring."

"Vision?" Jacob said gaining somewhat of an ounce of composure. "I don't care about a vision. I'll do whatever you want, just let me have this forever."

He could have screamed the words, but she moaned loudly and like a pop, Jacob went from being docile to an aggressive beast. Slamming himself forward heavily, he thrust harder with each stroke of his cock.

"Yes," she hissed into a moan.

Legs wrapped around him. Nails dig into his back. Teeth sunk into his shoulder. She gasped, cooed, and cried out. It egged him on. So much so that he boiled out an eruption of cum and still thrust like a mad man.

"Give me more," she cried out.

And he did. Not stopping for the cramp in his side. For how thirsty he felt. Not even for the fact that right now, the numbness of his cock had appeared but did nothing to abate how deep it penetrated. If anything, Jacob felt that he reached deeper now than he did a minute ago. Still, the inevitability of the flesh reached her.

She let out a harrowing screech before having a pleasure seizure underneath him. The flesh quivered and he leaned back a bit as he couldn't thrust or even move anymore. Her sex gripped and milked his cock and he joined her in orgasm with a powerful grunt. He collapsed onto her, feeling completely drained of strength. A warm feeling spread over him.

"That was amazing," he said between breaths.

"I agree," she moaned into his ear. It tickled, but he didn't make a move to show it. Instead, he let out a breath of contentment while he tried to fight off the wave of exhaustion washing over him. He failed and darkness soon swallowed his consciousness.

Black.

It is a color Jacob had grown to hate. His whole life had been black. From the blinding pains of being verbally hurt to the physical pains of a heavy fist. Black swallowed love completely out of his life. There was nothing and Jacob had felt like there was something.

Then a light appeared, bringing him once more into salvation. There, was the throne in front of him, but she wasn't there. No, instead she stood next to him.

"I haven't seen that throne before from this perspective," she commented.

"It's intimidating with all the stairs."

"All you have to do is go up them."

"Is it worth seizing?"

"Was bringing me here worth it?"

"Yes."

Jacob took a step forward towards the set of stairs. He felt invigorated with that one step.

"You normally step back," she commented. "Is it because you want to go forward now?" He took another step. A sudden heavy weight stopped him.

"Why can't I move anymore?"

"You aren't ready for more yet."

When will I be?

'When you are.

Jacob awoke suddenly with a startle. He was alone on the bed. His stomach growled and he yawned to it. Getting up, he wandered to the bathroom to relieve himself. He thought he needed a shower but instead stopped by his room to dress.

Moving through the house, he went downstairs to find the priestess in the kitchen. The fridge was open and she was currently going through it.

"What are you doing?" he asked her, not minding that he got a full view of her backside as she bent over in the fridge. Her fat pussy lips looked tantalizing as he stared at her sex.

"I'm hungry," she said.

"I can cook something," he offered as his cock twitched. Honestly, he wanted to bury his face into her sex right then and there, but both of them were hungry. "Or order something."

She came out of the fridge. Her form had changed again. This time, she sported a petite figure. Barely any curved or breasts.

"Why do you keep changing your frame?"

"Because I'm trying to find a perfect form for myself that I like. There are many different body types and I want to find the perfect one for my sexuality."

"Oh," he said noticing her eyes were a white color.

So what can we order?

He smiled and picked the phone up.

"Pizza sounds good?"

She cocked her head at him.

"Order it."

And she turned away from him before going back into the fridge. With a shake of his head, he ordered a few pizzas. Being modest at first with the order and hearing her munch away in the fridge, he called back and added a few more to the order. By the time he finished that, his ass wiggling while she rooted round got to him.

"I can't take it anymore," he yelled out grabbing his now throbbing cock. Jacob hoped the priestess remained unaware of him as he positioned himself behind her. Granted, she probably was aware, but he liked the fantasy that she was teasing him on purpose. Much to his delight, she responded as he slid into her.

"About time," she sighed. "I like the cold in the fridge and it made my nipples delightfully hard."

Jacob took her word for it, to engross on the suction of her cunt on his cock. The way the lips rolled over his phallus made him coo to himself in pleasure. Before long, he heard a cracking sound.

"Fuck me harder."

"I hear cracking," he responded not stopping even from a moment in concern for it really.

Suddenly, there was a splitting crack and she fell into the fridge.

"We have to stop," he said knowing that they had broken the shelves in the fridge.

"Don't you dare," she said, a growl coming from what felt like the depths of her pussy. That sound made him double his efforts on her. Desensitized with the third time of sex, Jacob marveled and smiled to himself with the sweat rolling above his brow. That was until a ringing doorbell.

"Shit, pizza is here."

Jacob peeled out of her and moved quickly pulling his shorts up. The doorbell rang again and he ran to the front door. Opening it up, Jacob let out a gasp of surprise.

"Kenny?"

"Jacob? Back to eating whatever whenever?"

Kenny was a small bully, not even a part of Billy's gang that tormented Jacob at school. No, Kenny was a bully that hunted the neighborhood and often looked for Jacob to hurt.

"Look man, just let me buy the pizza," Jacob replied.

"Oh you will, plus extra. I want a big tip."

"I'll pay what you deserve."

Jacob was shoved back into the house.

"No, you'll pay what I say you will."

Kenny put the pizza down n the floor and closed the house door.

Jacob is that the pizza?

Jacob looked back to see the priestess.

"What is going on?" She asked standing naked in the doorway of the kitchen.

"Well, well Jacob, what a surprise man.

"Get back," Jacob said to her. Suddenly a fist landed on his face.

"No one said to talk," Kenny yelled at him. Jacob heard a growl, but he blinked heavily through painful tears.

"Hey now there babe," Kenny said. "What's a fine-looking woman like you doing with a freak like him."

"You hurt him."

"Yeah, what of it."

"He can't be hurt."

"Yeah well, make it worth my while and I won't hurt him anymore."

"Okay."

Jacob knew already what was gonna happen. Even as the sounds of pants being dropped he knew whatever she did, it wouldn't end well for Kenny.

"Yeah that's right, open your mouth slut."

The sounds of slurping filled the air.

'Jesus Jacob, this bitch suck dome like a porn star.

Even though the comment made Jacob smile a bit and dulled the pain, he knew Kenny's joy would be short-lived. After all, Billy had a fun end after he hurt Jacob. Able to open his eyes now, he opened them to her sucking him off.

She was on the balls of her feet, knelt in front of him. His dick didn't appear at all. Her form had changed once again and now she was voluptuous. The thickness of her thighs made him want her again. Then he locked eyes with her, pink mixed with red. A finger held up and then Kenny began to scream.

A spray of blood erupted from Kenny's crotch, showering her with its blood. Kenny fell back against the door.

"Come on lover," she said to him. "Don't you want me still?"

"Get away from me you monster," Kenny screamed in utter terror at her.

"Well, I want more," she said looking over at Jacob.

It was a look of nightmares. Her chin had split at the bottom revealing rows of teeth. Teeth dripping with blood as it pooled on the floor below. The front of her was covered in it too. She held a hand up and her fingers elongated into tentacles. Kenny was whimpering by now.

"So much more."

Jacob didn't even see her move, but he heard the sickening sound of flesh being punctured. Kenny had fallen silent.

More.

He watched in morbid fascination as she moved over to Kenny. The sounds of flesh tearing and eating morbidly fascinated me. He heard her groan and moan and at that moment a thought came to him.

"Aurora," he said. She stopped tearing at the flesh to look over at him.

"Your name is Aurora."

"Why?" she asked.

"Such beauty but so deadly."

"And?"

"It was my mother's name."

She went back to tearing at the flesh. What started as a night of sex and love had turned into one of murder. Sure a few hours had passed, but by whatever god they worshipped, she looked erotically monstrous. He got up and walked over to a box of pizza.

After he moved over to sit against a wall, he sat down and began to eat himself in earnest. All the while listening to Aurora eat away. He wondered if naming her that particular name was a good fit.

Aurora had approached him as a motherly figure and quickly as an actual lover. Probably the most honest entity in his life, she had oozed sex at him from their first meeting. As he ate slice after slice of pizza, he felt happier with life now. Two bullies have gone and his dad was out of the picture for however long he decided to be, Jacob felt at peace.

And not because of the pizza he ate either. Food would always bring him happiness, but now, he had Aurora. Who now was munching on bones. A fact he asserted with the cracking sounds from her.

"Is it necessary to eat the bones?"

She stopped to look at him, a bone hanging out of her mouth. It dropped to the floor. "What am I supposed to do with it?"

"Leave it, we can dispose of it later, why not have some pizza instead?"

Jacob pointed at the boxes next to his corpse of Kenny.

"I'll dispose of it now."

She squeezed her breasts and much to his astonishment and enjoyment, black liquid shot out from her nipples. Immediately upon touching the flesh, a hissing sound filled the room as steam rose off the corpse. Squeeze after hard squeeze went until she turned to him.

"That should do it, now let me eat some of this pizza."

Aurora grabbed the five other boxes and sat next to Jacob on the wall. She began eating one of the pizzas before commenting.

"So this is pizza," she said.

"Yeah, good huh?"

"Better than the flesh," she said. "Who knew sex gave one such an appetite?"

It Burns a lot of calories.

"You really weren't all that popular huh?"

"Life has been hard," Jacob replied finishing off the current slice he was eating before starting on another. She had picked up a second box to begin eating. Jacob contemplated while he ate his current slice.

"Do you like it here?"

"It's okay so far. I really can't wait to see what you have planned for this place."

"It's gonna be difficult with my father."

She fell silent as she chewed on pizza.

"Maybe, but what if you bought me a place to stay?"

"Would you want that? Being away from me all the time?"

The third box going, he saw how fast she ate.

"You will visit every day," she said as a matter of fact.

"I can afford it, let me look. We are safe until my dad shows back up anyways."

"Or I can find a girl that can entice your dad into being so busy he wouldn't have time to worry about you."

"I don't know if I would want to reward my father with something like that." "Oh, it doesn't have to be a reward, more of a breaking. He's the worst to you right?"

"Yeah," Jacob replied getting up. He didn't particularly find himself interested anymore in discussing plans. Especially those revolving on getting his dad laid. That man was a monster.

Moving through the house, he went up to his bedroom. By now, the night had gotten late and he did know he needed to rest up. Starting up his computer, he looked at delivery dates and saw many of the newly ordered household items would be arriving tomorrow. Smiling, he got up to shower. After seeing the death and having sex multiple times that day, he needed another.

Getting into the shower, Jacob let the day wash off him. He was using an arm to support himself with great relief when the shower curtain ripped open.

"What are you doing?" he cried out with a jump.

"I'm covered in blood."

She got in the shower with him, and Jacob moved out of her way while she rinsed the blood off herself. The smell almost made him wretch. He looked away from her until he caught the scent of flowers. Opening his eyes, he realized at some point her soaps had been moved to his bathroom.

"You had to kill him?"

"Word gets out that you're fucking the hottest piece of ass in this material world and we will have more problems than you can count."

"He delivered pizza here."

She was silent for a moment.

"He did, and someone will come to visit. We will act normal. There is nothing they can find."

Jacob wasn't so sure. There was a record of the guy delivering. He was thinking when suddenly she had pushed her backside up against him and used her ass to press him back. The cold shower wall stopped him.

"What are you doing?"

"Getting closer and needing you to wash my breasts down."

She pulled his hands out and squirted some soap into them.

"Now, lather me up."

Breasts, as everything with women, were new to Jacob. Even though they had been sported by the three women he had the pleasure of being with, none had thus far offered their mammaries to him. He took to the task with tentative enthusiasm. Being slow to act with such enthusiasm thus far had seemed to serve him well.

The breasts were heavy and firm in his hands. Their form was bigger than when she had gotten into the shower with him. As he massaged the flesh, she moaned softly to him. Throughout everything though, he did notice she had inverted nippled.

"Why do you keep your nipples hidden?" he asked hotly into her ear.

"Not a big reason, but mostly because they are super sensitive and dangerous. I can swap between body fluids and to do that, I need protection for the nozzles." "Nozzles?" Jacob asked. He knew what she meant, but he did know that he wanted to find out exactly what her actual nipples were like. While she explained to him the different ones she sported. He lost interest quickly as he pushed fingers into the pouched that hid her nipples.

"What are you doing?"

"Washing."

She was panting and soon enough, he had the hard nubs of her nipples poking out of the mammaries. They were hard and felt like firm rubber in his hands. Hissing and gasps filled the air.

He became aware of his hard cock pressing between the cheeks of her ass.

"Want to do something with that?" she asked with a throaty moan.

"If you want it, have at it."

Her hands fell away from his and he felt her pull her ass cheeks apart. His cock found itself buried back into her.

"You don't need to move," she said. "I can handle the work, but don't stop what you're doing with my breasts."

He said nothing and instead did relax. Quickly, he learned what she meant was that she planned on grinding on him. Ass pressed up against him and cushioned them as she groaned, her heat slick as it molded itself around his length.

In moments she was spasming heavily in his arms. A surge of adrenaline hit Jacob and he took advantage of her weakened control and shoved her forward. Aurora let out a gasp of surprise as she fell into the torrent of rainwater, but Jacob stifled that into moans as he gripped her hips and drove himself relentlessly into her.

Their slapping bodies meeting with his thrusts seemed to echo in the bathroom. To the point that it almost deafened him. Eventually, the water got to him and he slung the shower curtain.

"Get your ass on the counter," Jacob said pulling himself out of her sex. She let out a protest but he slapped her ass. "Get on the counter faster and you can have it back."

She stood up in the shower, her eyes burning pink. A loom of astonishment hung on her face but she licked her lips.

"I like commands," she said moving out of the shower. Steam rolled off her and clung to the bathroom mirror. He throbbed in impatience as she got on the sink counter. Legs spread she told him to come to get it.

"Aren't you gonna pull your lips apart like before?" he asked.

"That was only to keep you in me for worship. Do you plan on pulling your cock out again?"

"No."

"Then stop fucking around and get that log of man meat back in me and rail my ass."

"Do you mean the figuratively or literally, cause I would like to fuck your ass soon," Jacob said before moving up to her. They happened to be at the perfect height for his cock to go into her eagerly waiting cunt. Their sex joined and even if he tried not to shove his cock as deep as he could immediately, he doubted her vaginal muscles would have allowed him to. Not that there was a complaint to have. Except maybe how sticky he was getting fucking her in the steam of the bathroom. Either way, he wasn't going to complain with his newfound fucktoy.

Aurora pulled him slowly to her and the change gave Jacob a naughty idea. He lifted her off the counter and found himself straining a bit from the effort. He lifted her and stepped back. In reaction, she wrapped her legs around him.

"Oh Jacob, you're strong," she cried out. He drove himself into her still and became aware of how slick the cunt had become. Moments more, she began shaking and he felt a warmness spread down his legs.

"Yeah and now I am really gonna need another shower."

"Sorry," she giggled. " I think that's only gonna get worse with the bodily fluids the longer you take to empty your balls into me."

"I have been trying, but they keep filling up fast than I can get it out."

"So much," she said digging nails into his shoulder. "Pent-up energy hasn't been good for you."

"I know, but your pussy is milking it any chance it feels like it."

"I do so love having sex," she said unwrapping herself from him and pulling away. "As much as I didn't want your cock out of me, I am gonna bend over the sink."

And she did. Even reached back and pulled her ass apart showing her dripping sex to him.

Come on Jacob, you make me wait too much.

With a smile, Jacob went plunged his worries away, not caring anymore how long it took to finish. What mattered to him, is that her cries for more never stopped, and neither did her encouragement.

Jacob cringed while he walked a bit. Sore or not, he walked normally despite the pain. A requirement he put on himself because of Aurora. Fear about what she would say kept him putting up with the pain.

The thought of her made him smile. She had been at him every chance she got. Providing more sex than probably most at any given time, but he was happy to get away for some respite. Problems would arise if he spent every moment he could fucking. His social life would suffer.

Not that there was a social life, to begin with. With no friends and little activity outside the home besides school, the home was all there was. No one called to check on him. Except for last night. His dad called.

That conversation went well enough. His father even seemed happy on the phone. Talks of travel and plans upon his return home. No mention of the emergency call, but Jacob knew that there wasn't a bone in the man's body that cared about his son. That didn't matter last night though as it normally would to Jacob. Aurora had been there, waiting to embrace him and take his care away. He stopped on the sidewalk at the thought of Aurora.

The sun sat in the sky, still low as it rose. With a yawn and stretch, he continued on his way to school. Running a few minutes early today, he wanted a head start for the day. It was Friday and his father would be home late the next day. A lot had to be done.

Aurora had now been in a feminine body for three days. That caused his dilemma as he realized that Aurora wanted to use that body in all capacities. That in itself she took no blame with a new physical form. Needs caused neglect of the other chores needing to be done.

All the furniture needed to be assembled and even though the patriarch wasn't loved, Jacob did feel like the shocks coming would be better taken with a better-looking furnished home.

Sighing, he started moving towards school once again.

The walk didn't take long now. When he was bigger, the walk would take him thirty minutes or longer to complete. Now, it took only ten minutes. He wanted a thirty-minute window alone to check on Grace.

About a week ago, she had made a move on Jacob and the two had fucked in one of the many hiding places on the high school campus. Since then, he visited every morning to see the pulsating cocoon that contained her.

Jacob asked Aurora why Grace changed. Aurora skirted the question, but mostly assured him it was for the better. There would also need to be more. The spreading of knowledge about the Goddess of Love and Lusts would bring a better world. Jacob accepted the answer, but still found himself bothered by it.

The doors of the school were almost always opened early. Teachers did arrive before students. Most of those teachers rarely even noticed Jacob walking through the halls. Many, if not all knew Jacob had little to go home to so they turned blind eyes. But that was all before he lost the weight.

Now as he walked in, many teachers did look up. A few even said some greetings to him. One way or another, he didn't think any of them really cared. Except for Grace, who Jacob barely saw as she slipped around a corner. That confounded him being that yesterday she had been still cocooned in one of the buildings next to the baseball field.

Moving rather quickly through the hall, he moved lightly to stay quiet. A feat that never would have been possible before. He felt like a rogue, moving through shadows and whatnot. It wasn't lost on him that the halls of the school were well-lit.

'Jacob," A harsh but silent voice said.

It stopped him dead in his tracks.

He turned to see Ms. Devons looking up at him with her blue eyes boring into him. Today, the woman was wearing black-rimmed glasses and had her hair pulled back into a bun. Her black pants suit is only offset by the dark blue blouse underneath a suit jacket.

"What do you think you're doing running through the hall of this school?"

"I uh," Jacob was at a loss as to what to say to her. It's not like he had a real reason that would make sense to her. Explaining that he was pursuing a woman he had fucked a week ago and had turned into a cocoon and now emerged didn't feel like a good story.

"Come with me now," she said harshly. Pulling him by the arm, she yanked him into a classroom. the heavy metal door being closed behind him made him worry.

He turned to look at her. Saw that the room walls were lined with colorful posters with literature saying printed on them. This classroom belonged to her.

"I can't believe you would do such a thing, Jacob," she yelled at him.

"That's enough," he said with an equally powerful voice. "You are one to talk about what's acceptable or not."

"What do you mean?" she said moving back against the door in the door.

"Grabbing a student's cock in his pants," Jacob said. The switch happened again. A surge of confidence swelled in him. Of course, he referred to the time he had knocked her down to get to the building where he would fuck Grace a week ago. When the teacher had reached up to gain purchase to stand, her hand had grabbed onto his dick.

"That was an accident," she said turning bright red. He knew then, that this whole thing had been a farce.

"Was it now?"

He took a step towards her.

"If you wanted to see it, all you had to do was ask."

With a zipper quickly down, Jacob pulled his massive cock out for Ms. Devons to see. She gasped at the sight, an audible look of horror on her face.

"Much bigger than you thought huh?"

"What happened to you?" she asked. But he could see by her slight fidgeting that that question didn't matter in its intent.

"A teacher grabbed it. Want to feel it bare this time?" he asked holding out it towards her. Even though they were a few feet apart, he hoped the offer would still be tantalizing for her. He could use some relief.

"I," she looked around the room. "I think we have only a few minutes. Would a taste be okay?"

Jacob smiled at that. And she was over to him and on her knees. There were some mutterings of marveling, but her hot breath on his skin left him little to think about.

Is there a way I can study this later?" she asked.

He looked down at her beaming blue eyes and felt disappointed.

"I thought you said we had a few."

"We do," she replied standing up. She moved over to the door and leaned against it. "My pants are loose enough so they'll slide down past my ass. Get them down and come shove that thing up into me."

Bounding over, almost skipping, Jacob did as she commanded. Gripping the bands of her pants, he pulled until they popped over her ass and stopped at her thighs.

"That's far enough," she said. "Now stick it in."

"A good student obeys his teachers right?"

Jacob wanted to imagine that when he pulled her pants down, slick pussy juices would be thick. He imagined that they would be stuck to cloth and skin alike. There wasn't time to find out, but thankfully, she was wet enough for sliding right on in.

"Oh god," she cried out. A hand reached back and pulled on an ass cheek. It didn't matter to him. He was all happy to get closer to her heat.

"So much for needing a break," he said to himself.

"What was that?" she said with a moan.

"Your pussy is really hot," he shouted out, half-expecting some sort of panic on her part. There wasn't to his disappointment, but he shifted his thoughts to her sex.

She wasn't as tight as he would have liked, no doubt to her sexual activities. Mattering a little, he began shoving his cock deep as he could into her.

Ms. Devons whimpered in the onslaught. Cock shoved up against her womb, Jacob did his best to keep her womb kissing the tip of his dick. That was until she started meeting his thrust and then he found he didn't need to try so hard.

"You're a screamer huh?" Jacob said between exerted breaths.

"Yeah, and it's really hard to keep quiet," she said with gasps. Thankfully, Jacob didn't need to hear her scream. What he needed was to cum. That desire seemed to take over, but then the bell rang.

"No," she let out a groan of despair. They had both stopped. "I have to get ready for class. Students will be here soon."

They uncoupled and within seconds, both of them had their respective pants back up.

"You have detention on Monday young man," she said to him. "While I can say I enjoyed this, you will need to pay for the running in the halls."

"Yeah, okay," he said with a laugh. "See you Monday after school."

Jacob left the class. He knew the first bell was only a fifteen-minute warning until students started showing up in droves. Even though they could have continued, each second after the bell would be one to discover faster. And no teacher wanted to be caught with a student, even if that student was of age.

With a shrug, he moved back to the hall he last saw Grace move down. Even though people would be arriving by the minute, he still found himself needing to know where she was off too.

Moving slowly, not wanting to be caught up again by another teacher, he listened. The hall Grace had been last seen going down did have a dead end. So he moved slowly until he heard a sound. An unexpected and throaty moan.

Now Jacob moved quicker. Another moan and he knew which classroom it was. Room 606, which was funny being that the room was always vacant. Used for extra storage, it was no wonder why Grace would have used the room to masturbate in. Laughing a bit to himself at his worry, he knew the woman had a major sex drive and a few days without relief. Might have a rapacious sex drive like Aurora.

Opening up the door, Jacob expected to see Grace spread eagle on the floor going to town on herself. Maybe even shoving some sort of object inside to simulate. What he didn't expect to see was her riding someone.

"Close the door, if you want to join, just take your pants off," she said.

"Grace," Jacob replied horrified at what he saw.

Grace had in fact, emerged from her cocoon changed. Tentacles sprouted from her back. They looked to be sucking on arms and legs. He closed the door softly and walked over.

"Hey Jacob," she said to him, flipping her hair back. Closer, he saw that it too was a mass of tentacles. He moved around to see her from the front. Everything about Grace screamed that she was now of another world. "Like what you see?"

"No," he said. "What are you doing?"

"Fucking," she said. "Well, more like riding. This has been a more one-sided tryst that I wanted."

Her solid blue eyes looked at him.

'Want to join?

He did, but he knew it was a bad idea.

"Who is it?"

"Mr. Watts, I think. I don't know if it matters really. He won't be around for much longer."

"You can't do that," he said with a harsh whisper.

"You're beginning to throw off my high of this," she said, eyes narrowing at him.

"I'm not trying to."

"Then get your cock out and give me some," she hissed. A tentacle wrapped around his leg.

"I want to Grace, but the time."

"Means nothing. Get it out now."

Too afraid now not to say something he told her to knock it off.

"Look at the poor man you're killing him and at school. People saw him this morning and will ask questions when he isn't in class. Get off him now," he commanded.

There was a look of surprise on Grace's alien-looking face as her body reverted to human form. She still had Mr. Watts's cock in her as she straddled him. That man looked worse for wear. Submerged in water for too long, he was wrinkled head to toe. Nothing about his breathing looked like it was easy.

"How did you do that?"

"Do what?"

"You shut my need for sex completely off. I fuck this man almost every day and you made me stop. He has such a good cock."

"You were eating him," Jacob said.

A look of disgust came across her face.

"It felt so good though," she said. "To have such complete control of every bit of this." "Well, you don't know. You need to get dressed and get to work."

"What about him?" she asked standing up. Jacob's eyes raised seeing the thick trunk of a cock fall out of her. Not long, but thicker than a wrist.

"He isn't dead so leave him for now. Meet me at my house later."

"Okay," she said biting her lip.

"No sex either until we work out what to do."

"Until you work out to do," she said with a pout. "I mean, I need some cock. You know how hard it's gonna be to wait?" "You don't think I know that. I want to fuck you here and right now, but we have a responsibility here not to get exposed. What would our queen think?"

Grace seemed to pale with the statement.

"You're right," she said with a defeated tone. "I will keep control until I can find a more suitable partner."

"Get dressed," he commanded. The second bell rang, signaling the true arrival of the student body.

She did and to no surprise, she put on a white sundress with light blue flowers and trims. While dressing, Jacob looked at Mr. Watts. Poor man's wizened breath made him look terrible. As he studied, Jacob could see that she had sucked the man almost down to the bone. His ribs were looking visible.

"You did a number on him," Jacob said with disappointed dissidence.

"He agreed to the price, and I was hungry."

She stretched.

"You better get to class there kiddo."

With a sigh, he moved to leave the class. She grabbed him on his way by and planted a kiss on him. With soft lips, she moved the dead mood into one of the wonderful promises.

"Why would you do this?" he asked angrily.

If I have to suffer," she said with a gleam in her eyes. "So do you.

Then she left, leaving him throbbing in the departure. Sighing again, he followed but by the time he entered the hall, she had fallen into the crowd of students that had gathered. Frustrated for the second time that day, Jacob clunked off to his first class.

Classes for Jacob were often slow. Billy had been a constant torment, but he was gone now. Sure, people talked about him and even asked where he could be, but no one directed attention to Jacob for these things. Not that he had anything to do with Billy's death. That unfortunate incident had everything to do with Aurora's protectiveness than anything else.

The day went fast. There wasn't much in classes and most people offered little to him.

He did pass Ms. Devons throughout the day, who blushed heavily each time they crossed paths. Once she tried to avoid looking at him. Another, they got close in the class and he grabbed her butt as he passed. She let out a squeak of protest.

That made him laugh to himself as he wondered on his way to auto shop class how she even kept herself sane. Somehow, or rather, he knew, her pussy was gestating all day. It made him jittery imagining that she would be rubbing her slit all day in various ways to stimulate herself.

Finally, the last bell rang. Everyone avoided him still. He did eye a few girls looking at him, but under the gaze, they turned quickly away. Getting up, Jacob went to leave when he was stopped.

"Jacob," the teacher for the day said in a stern voice. It was Mr. Davids. A rather lanky teacher who often subbed in for teachers when he could. He was one of the track coaches and a counselor by trade.

'Yeah?" he replied standing at the doorway.

The older man looked at Jacob. Everyone knew Mr. Davids was fresh out of college and he looked young. That being said, the man commanded some respect for his authority. That stopped Jacob being that his cock throbbed insistently to be buried in a Ms.

Devons snatch and finish what started earlier.

"So it's freaky what happened with you."

"Yeah."

"You gonna explain?"

Jacob thought for the second time of telling someone what really transpired. That made him wonder for a second if maybe there existed in a way, something inside wanted him to tell. Everything was for the Goddess now, but he had no name to tell. The lack of details justified not telling.

"Just melted off," he said.

"Bull kid," Mr. Davids replied. "I don't know what you did but miracles don't happen."

They did if the thing fucking your brains out constantly was a life form from another plane of existence. But Jacob didn't say that. He couldn't.

"I saw a doctor, they were baffled by this too," he said with a shrug.

Davids nodded at this explanation and then turned away. Jacob wasted no time in the opening and slipped out the door. Ms. Devons awaited him and he needed to get at that pussy.

Walking briskly through the halls, he half-expected to be stopped. As he went, nothing was stopping him from her classroom. Upon entering he found himself disappointed to see that she was engaged with a parent. It took seconds for him to learn that the parent was unhappy about her child's grades. He locked eyes with Ms. Devons.

At that moment, he knew she would be more than a few minutes. Those eyes also seemed to plead with him to wait. He nodded at her and he saw the slight bite of a lower lip.

"Sorry Ms. Devons, wanted some help with homework. I'll be waiting down in room, 705," he said before turning and walking briskly away.

Room 705 was the room where Grace had been feeding on the male teacher from earlier. Jacob did hope the guy was okay, but as he opened the door to see clothes still strewn on the floor, his heart sank.

"You should let me finish him off," a female voice said. Jacob turned to see Grace leaning against the wall next to the door. "He would have died better."

"I forgot," Jacob said sheepishly.

"And now instead of dying in a sweet embrace, he died wheezing and alone."

"Why were you feeding on him?"

"I was hungry and he couldn't keep up."

"Keep up?"

"Oh, he wasn't like you. I needed more orgasmic bliss with him and more bonding time. His body gave out long before we bonded."

Is this how it's going to be with every convert?" Jacob said with an exasperated sigh.

"We require certain things to have for a mate. Everything is for the Goddess, but to continue to be worthy, all have to meet requirements. He did not, and as such, he worshipped only once."

The matter-of-fact explanation satisfied him for the moment. It seemed that there were a lot of things worth discussing with Aurora. If he managed to keep converting women, having them wander and eat any male they came across until they found a mate caused too many problems. Three had been killed so far in the endeavors of two different alien women.

"There need to be some ground rules," he said.

"Well, first, let's do something about the hard cock in your pants," she said with a moan. Her hand lifted her dress and another went to town on an audibly wet pussy. "At least you could let me ride that good hard dick for a long while."

"I can't," he replied with a solemn grimace.

"I know, there is another about to join our fold. I don't think she would mind, but by the off chance."

Grace was moaning much more audibly now.

"Why are you doing that?"

"Because our new convert needs all the help she can get to accept the changes heading her way. Pheromones will lull her into an easier change. Your cock will do most of the work, as she has already tasted its goodness."

Fuck it," Jacob said with growing frustration.

Jacob walked up to her and yanked her hand out of her pants. She went to protest, but he shoved the musky fingers into her mouth. Blue eyes looked at him. She licked the finger seductively slow. At that moment, Jacob unzipped his pants and yanked his cock out. His next action had him lifting her leg.

"That's right," she groaned into his ear. "Shove that fat cock into my tight little cunny."

He grunted in reply. Shoving his cock into her with dominating force, going until she began shuddering.

"That hit the spot," she said with a sigh.

"You came already?"

"Yeah," she said, the word was drawn out and sounded like a drunk spoke.

Jacob watched as she lost composure of the form she held. Her skin paled and her hair tentacled. He watched as her lower jaw split into the middle and rows of pointed teeth showing. Light blue spots began to appear on her as they would be on a cow. Not that she was a cow, far from it.

"She will be here any second," he said worried about her appearance.

"I will hide shortly, just let me finish orgasming."

Jacob hadn't realized it, but her pussy still squeezed his cock in long waves. It almost made him want to finish what he started with her. He could almost feel how heavy his balls had become with their hanging weight. The insistent throbbing in the head of his cock told him his body grew impatient with the delayed end.

"You can pull out now," she said plainly to him. And he did. A long slide out and he heard a splash on the floor. "Jeez, you make me so wet you know?"

Within seconds, Grace looked like herself again. Jacob pulled his pants back up and got his cock back in.

"You need to leave," Jacob said zipping himself up.

"I know," Grace replied. "You take a lot out of a girl, and she is coming down the hallway."

"You need to hide," Jacob said with panic.

"I will," she said with a sigh.

Jacob looked panicked at the door when it opened. He didn't see Grace move or anything as Mrs. Devons walked in.

"Jacob?"

"I'm here," Jacob said. One of the things he hadn't given credit to anything was how gloomy the room was. It did have windows, but with blinds and stacked desks, the room often sat in a permeating dinginess. Near dark is where the room needed to be anyways for the secrecy it provided, especially in the late with all of the extra activities for it.

"Oh thank goodness," she said closing the door behind her. "Even though you told me I was nervous you wouldn't be here."

"Why?" he asked her.

"We don't have time for that, I need your cock now."

Jacob opened his arms wide. A microphone for her to declare her lustful enrollment into servitude. Time seemed to stop as she moved over to him. Dropping in front of him, he closed his eyes as her hands pulled his throbbing rod out.

It smells so musky," she said.

"Sorry been a long day."

Eyes still closed and making no movements, he waited until she made another move. That wait didn't take long her mouth wrapped around his cock. With a gurgling moan, the sounds of slurping filled the room. The slurping would continue, promising a greedy appetite and sloppy sex. He shuddered when a powerful vacuum engulfed his length.

Jacob looked down to eyes peering up at him. Ms. Devons seemed to smile before she closed her eyes. Head bobbing, Jacob lasted exactly a few seconds more before grunting out a finish.

Coughing brought him out of the orgasmic bliss. He looked down to see Ms. Devons coughing into her hands.

"You okay?"

"Yeah," she said between some coughs. "Just a lot more than I expected."

"The cock or cum?" Jacob asked with a laugh.

"Both I suppose," she said standing up. Lips smacking she looked at him. "That was some thick stuff."

"Sorry," he said with a shrug.

"I want some of it in my..."

Go ahead, say it.

A look passed across her face. He couldn't tell if it was disgust or conflict. It wouldn't matter as she smiled quickly.

"I need you to put some of that thick spunk in my pussy," she said with a squeal.

He smiled at her and dropped his arms.

"Whatever you need."

Ms. Devons moved over to one of the desks stored in the room. She pulled a wooden office chair out. Pants dropped to the floor, filling the room with the musk of wanton lust. A leg hiked up on the chair and spreading of one ass cheek, which showed dripping lips and a peculiar color of sex to Jacob. Heavy brown-looking lips draped down with copious amounts of juices dripping from them. Looking carefully, he could see shimmering strings stretching too, to the panties on the floor below. Not needing any more of an invitation, Jacob waltzed up to the alter of worship.

"Best part of you younger ones is that you recharge fast."

Jacob caught himself asking how many of the older women at the school would know such a thing.

She groaned throatily as he slid into her heat. The angle made her tighter, but he didn't get to savor the feeling of vaginal walls molding to him. Hips began moving before he sank in all the way and it felt more to him as if she took control of the impaling.

"I've been thinking of this cock all day," she exclaimed shoving herself back harder.

"Good cause the pussy has been on its mind all day."

Can you thrust harder?

The question made him pause for a second.

"What did you say?"

"Can you thrust harder?"

"How dare you slut," he angrily growled. He grabbed her head, fingers entwining into her hair.

"Yes," she screamed out when he pulled her hair. With a final push back, she froze.

There was no movement, and Jacob stayed still. Though he wondered what transpired right then, he dare not interrupt it. While her heart and ass pressed against him, he listened to her breathing.

Moments stretched to what seemed like minutes. An eternity could pass at the moment and Jacob wouldn't know when it would end. Even though he was aware of her heartbeat and his own cock's insistence, he did not move. Sighing to himself, life seemed to stop completely. Then it changed, and the pause button was unpressed.

"Fuck yes," Ms. Devons screamed out. Jacob was taken aback by the sudden animation. Flesh shaking, ass cheeks flexing ad they spread with pushing back. A wall stopped his cock from going in further, but he felt the pulsations in her cumming cunt.

"I accepted, oh I accepted."

Ms. Devons shoved Jacob away, to which he felt a bit indignant about having his hard cock yet again ripped out of pussy before it came.

'What the hell?" he said angrily.

Ms. Devons had gone too far to acknowledge him. Like a faucet running, black ichor poured out of her pussy in wet sloppy plops. As with Grace and Aurora, that ichor began growing tendrils of pure lack that snaked like veins up Ms. Devons' legs. She fell out of the chair and into the puddle of goo.

"Well done," Grace said, stepping seemingly out of the shadows. In the bit of light, there was, Jacob could see a grin on her face as she watched the conversion. "In three days, I will have a sister."

"Yeah," Jacob said, watching as the womb encompassed the teacher. In seconds, tentacles snaked out for the anchoring and defense. "We are gonna have to lock the room up."

"For her?" Grace said with a laugh. "Anyone who wonders in here will be kept alive until she emerges."

"And she will emerge hungry," he said.

"And horny," she replied. "And speaking of horny, you want to fire that thing off into my ass?"

"Tempting, but right now, I just want to go home."

"Oh."

"Let's get out of her first, the noises of this transformation are almost sickening."

"It's a song of beauty," Grace said. Jacob couldn't tell if rebuke or statement wove into the words. With a shrug, he pulled his pants up and fixed himself.

Still, let's get home.

'You're denying me a chance to worship?

Grace started into him about the rebuke of sex from earlier. While he understood her insistence on taking care of sex, the timing would be off. None of this mattered to Grace. She wanted more and he denied her.

They walked the halls of the school together, not coming across another soul as they did. Jacob would have liked to talk about that, not knowing how late it was. Instead, they walked with her repeating the same plea. Eventually, they passed the office and she told him she needed to get something out of her office. He followed and realized before the door to her office even closed, that he would be fucking her.

"Now then," Grace said.

Jacob moved quickly and shoved her up against the door. It interrupted whatever thought she planned on presenting. Hard and desperate again for his own release, he lost caring about holding off.

"What-?" "You want to be fucked in the ass, well, you got it."

Pulling her dress up, he moved his cock out at the same time, each hand working while he used his weight to hold her. With the tasks done, his cock sprang angrily into the cleft of her ass.

"You don't need any-oh, you know."

Jacob did. The converts would always be ready for any orifice to be used. Somehow he knew this and would never now forget it.

'Yes, slide it in deeper.

Jacob did, feeling the ring of her ass a tight barrier that constantly squeezed down his shaft. Like a rolled o-ring up and down a pipe. It didn't take long for her to lose her composure again.

Grace's alien form sprang into existence before his eyes. Not that it bothered him. By now, pleasure overrode everything else as he rutted to a finish.

"Fuck," Grace called out with a cracking sound punctuating the outcry. He could tell she was cumming, but didn't stop shoving his cock hard into her. The thrusts' feverish pace were met now as

Grace threw herself back into him. "You're taking too long, give me your cum."

The begging picked up there. He didn't know what had gotten into her, besides his dick, but that begging made him feel powerful. At a whim, he could end the sex by emptying into the bowels of her ass. A whim, that he continued to shove his cock into her.

"I will cum when I am good and ready too," she yelled over her begging. "Now turn your ass over."

Grace may have groaned, but it was on unhearing ears. To Jacob, all she needed to do was obey. Much to his delight, she swiveled herself and after some awkward repositioning, to which his cock never left her ass, they were back to fucking.

"Oh this is different," Jacob said looking into the blue galaxy eyes of Grace. With eyes locked with him, she licked her lips. A thick tongue that rolled over slowly.

"I'll say," she said her mouth agape now, exposing rows of sharp teeth. He looked down to watch her anus swallow his cock. The orifice stretched out like a volcano being plugged. After each pull-out, her pussy squirted a small stream of milky white spray.

Almost like a refined mist, and the color evident only by the streams that pooled off his cock. The extra lube made a squishy noise as the muscles clenched onto his cock.

Their eyes locked. He wanted to know what she thought. To even feel what her body felt. Everything for him lay at the shaft of his cock. That is until he felt the powerful throbs of inevitable for him.

"Do it," she said with a hiss. "Fill my ass up with you thick cream."

He groaned.

"Come on master, cum in my ass."

"Ah."

"Master, yes," Grace exclaimed. Powerful legs wrapped around his waist and held him tight against at his final thrust.

Jacob doubled over as his balls emptied with explosive ferocity. Each pump of cum made him heave with a spasm.

"Oh, that is so delicious."

Jacob looked up to see her licking her lips. A gloss seemed to cover her eyes.

"I can feel its warmth," she said falling back onto the desk completely. Her tentacles writhed around her on the desk as she relaxed. When her legs fell away, he pulled out of her ass.

"Warn a girl."

Sorry.

Jacob pulled his pants back up and made himself decent.

"We need to go."

"Yeah, I know."

Grace was slow to rise. When she did, he stared at her alien form.

"What?"

"You need to look human."

"Oh."

Only a second would pass for her to change.

"I can't wait till when I don't have to revert," she said looking at him. "It unnerves me that I can't be in my natural form."

He shrugged before motioning to the door.

"I need to get home," he said.

"You don't need to wait for me."

"I think I do. If you decide to snack on the way home."

She laughed.

"If I do, I'll behave. I do need clothes anyways so I will drop you off. I can't stay over at your place. It is the weekend."

She winked at him walking by. Jacob already knew that her promise would be broken. Not that he knew about her nightly dealings before she hooked up with him. What he did know is that her sex drive couldn't have been satiated.

They walked down the halls in relative silence. Grace was humming and doing a bit of a skip while they did. He thought the look was great but remembered that only in reality, that there would never be settling with her. In fact, as the main conduit to the Goddess with recruitment, many women would be in his future.

When they got outside, Grace kissed him and gave him thanks. With an apology, she left him standing in front of the school. Sighing heavily Jacob began the walk home.

Nothing happened on the walk home. There wasn't a constant bully anymore and the sinking sun provided a nice companion. Thoughts of the rest of the night filled his head. A shower had to be first on the list. Or a better idea would be to order food and then get a shower. He bet Aurora had eaten everything in the house.

When he arrived home, the boxes containing the ordered furniture sat still on the front porch. There were a ton of boxes. Sighing, he realized those needed to be moved in before a shower.

Jacob hardly ever felt at home. Not since his mother had passed and his father's abusive nature began. When he opened the door, the last thing he expected to see home greeting.

"Jacob."

His name was said on a wind of excitement. An embrace unexpected and coupled with strength. Tentacles hair wrapped around his head before wet lips crushed against his. Hot breath heralded the tongue that intermingled into his mouth. The kiss was long and passionate in its unexpected desperation.

"You've been having sex," Aurora said breaking the kiss with a giggle. "I can taste them on you."

"I'm sorry," Jacob said panicked.

"Why?" she asked looking up at him. Her pink eyes seemed to be sparkling.

"It isn't normal in my world for a woman to be excited about her man having sex with others."

"You were worshiping and recruiting. Any woman should be proud of her man's devotions."

She let him go.

"Are you coming in?"

"I need to bring the furniture in and start getting it ready."

"Your dad will be home tomorrow," she said with a twirl. "I can't wait to meet him."

The sharp tooth smile she wore on her face was one of utter horror. Her eyes were pools of red and then the look disappeared.

"I'm hungry."

"Chinese?"

"And you."

Let me order and I'll get to work on the furniture.

He knew she was watching him as he moved. An effort on his part to ignore it for now. There would be time later for her, but he needed to get things done.

Ordering the Chinese food proved to be challenging as he had to guess what quantities of food to order. The man on the phone seemed to be upset with how much was ordered, but Jacob promised a good tip to the delivery driver.

After the call, Jacob started unpacking boxes outside and moving furniture inside. Some had to be built, and he found a perverse sense of pride in himself when he finished bookshelves, various benches, new tables, and whatnot.

The only break he took was to eat. Aurora ate with him, but said little, her pink eyes locking with his often. Once done, he went right back to work, breaking down boxes, arranging furniture, and hanging pictures.

There wasn't much in the way of family in the house. Jacob couldn't even think of where to look even for old family photos when he ordered. Instead of relying on that, he decided to order many different art pieces involving the woods. As the woods had been such an escape for Jacob, it felt right.

All on the walls, he had pictures hung. Above the fireplace, he mounted a huge tv. Everything looked great and he fell with a huge sigh on one of the couches. No sooner had he done that, than Aurora was there.

"I thought you would never be done," she said sitting on the ottoman in front of him. He had his head back and made no effort to look at her.

"It was a lot," he said.

'Watching you work was something.

His head rolled up from the back of the couch. She was wearing some of the clothes he bought in her human form.

"I'm not sure what that means."

"It means you deserve some attention."

Aurora stood up in front of him.

"I learned a lot on your computer today. I thought I'd give you a treat."

Jacob remained silent. Not that he needed to say anything. She blew a kiss at him.

"Hope you're ready."

A smile broke across his face. She smiled back and then began to dance. There were twirls, leg kicks, and hands that moved across the body. Each movement is meant to bring out desire. Once clothes began moving and exposing skin, Jacob realized what the dance was for.

His cock strained almost immediately watching Aurora. Her fluid movements in dance are a choreographed masterpiece. Before long, skin became even barer as clothes were discarded. Eroticism at its finest, Jacob found his mouth agape as her pants fell.

The masturbation began in earnest at that point. Jacob didn't even see at first as their hands moved. What clued him in was the shimmering of liquid across her body coupled with the sweet smell of her salty sex. The moans she emitted eventually were drowned out by the sound of her wet sex being played with.

"Jacob," she moaned squeezing her breasts with a throaty moan. "Jacob, watching you was so infuriatingly hard to keep me from you."

Jacob had leaned forward towards her in not only intrigue but to touch. Reaching out, her warm body folding into his arms and he hugged her, hands on her butt and face buried into her stomach. Heartbeats heard, and he found a bit of comfort resting against her.

"I can't do it anymore," she said with a frustrated growl.

Jacob found himself on his back, pants ripped off and Aurora straddling him. The heat of her sex radiated out with a dripping insistence. There also was a sound of her still masturbating with the coupling of moans.

"I hope you are ready Jacob," she said, her voice flat.

Aurora stood up and lowered herself downwards to his erect penis. They locked eyes, she's furiously dark pink.

"Watch."

He looked down at the plump pussy lips, fat and engorged. Then pink tentacles snaked slowly out.

"Watch as they engulf your cock," she said. He could see the shudder of her body as the warm prehensile appendages wrapped around his cock. "Each one of those is more sensitive than any human woman's clitoris."

As if to emphasize, he watched as a milky white fluid dripped copiously from her sex. It may have grossed out anyone else, but Jacob knew it was a sign that Aurora was orgasming. He had been coated head to toe before in her juices. By now, it had become a bit of a ceremony to get his cock coated in her before they copulated.

"And let me tell you, Jacob," she said sinking down his shaft fully. "This amount of pleasure would be enough to drive any mortal mad."

Jacob grabbed her ankles, knowing the next bit would be rough. Unlike the other women who allowed Jacob to have his way with them for the most part, Aurora often over the past week had essentially been in control.

"You're so deep in me," she exclaimed with a moan.

And he felt like he was. Jacob at one point wanted to take the chance to study her anatomy. No doubt, that would involve him having to ask or forcing it. Aurora didn't seem to want to take things slow.

"Don't hold back Jacob," she demanded as fingers dug into his chest. Aurora grated, even more, leaning back so he had to look up at her heaving chest. She had lost control of her form, and her breast size had begun increasing. Not that it would matter. Any size would be perky and Aurora liked hers to be melons.

The next thing that changed with Aurora was her hair which combined and twirled into lengthy tentacles. Her nipples, around the areoles, sprouted tendrils too, which he knew to be overly sensitive.

"I'm gonna cum again," she cried out, going rigid. The spray of milky cum up his body. The explosion of female cum wasn't gross at all to Jacob. In actuality, he reveled in any woman's orgasm. For this one, he stuck his tongue out and enjoyed the sweet taste of it. She, of course, was shaking with massive spasms as each powerful vaginal contraction happened. The uncontrolled contractions of her cunt forced Jacob over his edge.

"Ah yes, fill me," Aurora screamed, her voice going into a high pitch. When she finished, she collapsed backward, popping his cock out of her. It sprang up, bringing with it, a mix of cum.

'That was wonderful.

"Yeah," Jacob agreed to listen to her labored breathing. He looked down at her spread legs to see her pussy splayed open. There weren't any tentacles anymore. Fat lips splayed apart where the nub of a huge clit sat and the dark hole of her pleasures.

"Like what you see?"

"I want to see more."

She laughed.

"You will, but for now, I have to get this body satisfied."

"What do you mean by that?" Jacob asked worried the sex for her wasn't wholesome. "What I mean is that I constantly crave sex and right now I struggle with control."

That made him think of Grace from earlier.

"What did you do today?"

"Do you mean who?"

"Yeah."

Jacob felt as if she was about to answer, but then a pounding on the door interrupted their conversation.

"Who could that be?" Jacob scrambled up. He quickly moved to find something to wear. Had to run upstairs to change quickly. Two more times the pounding on the door had happened.

"Hold on," Jacob said almost angrily on the fourth pound. He opened the door to see the blonde cop from earlier in the week.

"Can I help you, officer," he said trying to be cordial and sweet to her.

"Yeah, just checking in on you," she said. A radio crackled on her hip. She didn't pay any attention to it.

"I returned the cart," he said to her, not understanding one bit, why he felt like the spotlight was on him. This woman had an aura of power about her.

"I bet," she laughed. "You seem to have been busy."

"Yeah," he said, leaning back a bit as she looked into the house. He didn't think there was anything for him to worry about with a cop. Granted, he did know she was scoping the place out.

"Jacob, who is it?"

"It's the police Aurora."

That was a cue for Aurora, who arose from the couch with a long stretch. A white tank top did little to hide her body, which she wore as a stacked nubile woman.

"Everything okay?"

Jacob knew what the effort on Aurora's part was for. A seduction did get another convert. Not that he minded. The cop's looks were great and she did seem to have a personality that would allow for good expansion of the cult.

'Yeah, Officer?

"It's Officer Hadley. Meredith Hadley," she replied. "And yes, everything is okay."

"Is she thirsty?"

Aurora's question took him aback. The look on the officer's face was hard. Maybe she was concerned, but then she responded.

"Yes, can I have a glass of water?"

Jacob stepped aside and Meredith came in.

Jacob sat on the sofa, unsure of what was going on. Covered in sweat, tears, and bodily fluids, he sat back on the couch trying to catch his breath. Two women lay near him. Aurora with her curvaceous butt lay on the ottoman in front of the couch. From where he sat, he could see the glistening of moisture on her skin as well as the red swollen vulva.

The other woman, a female cop named Meredith, had been sucked into the night's events by Aurora. The cop lay on the floor after collapsing a few moments ago. Jacob found her screaming orgasms entertaining and they made him feel powerful. Aurora had passed out about an hour ago.

The scene looked serene now to him as he sighed in contentment. His cock felt warm and even as it dropped in exhausted flaccidity. He could even feel the post-coital drippage sliding out of his cock. If the tendrils of sleep didn't tug at him, worry of the mess created by the coupling would surely be there instead. In fact, Jacob's drowsiness quickly dissipated as two realizations hit him.

Meredith would change soon. There would be no doubt about that. A change brought on by him and whatever afflicted him for the Goddess. Soon the cop would cocoon and emerge as a devoted daughter of lust. But in the meantime, she would need a place to do such a thing and his house wouldn't be it.

The second realization concerned Aurora. This night happened to be the first that Jacob outlasted the sexual being. That reflection brought a smile to his face.

Getting up slowly, Jacob walked over to the woman. Kneeling, he placed a hand on her shoulder and gave it a push.

"Meredith."

The name and push were repeated a few times before Meredith stirred.

"What?" she asked groggily turning over.

"It's time to go," he replied.

The woman looked at him, eyelids drooping down.

"Okay."

That's all she said, before getting up slowly. Jacob moved away and surveyed the room. The cop's clothes were everywhere, but the woman made no effort to get them as she stood up. Instead, he heard the jingle of keys and watched as she wobbled naked out the front door. In seconds, the sound of a car starting and driving away filled the air.

"She left quick," he said.

"I know," Aurora groaned signifying her waking awareness. She rolled on the ottoman. Studying her for a moment, he watched in morbid fascination as her bone structure shifted immensely. Now at this moment, she wore a lithe body with massive breasts.

Why do you shift your form like that?

"I like to experiment," she said with a stretch. Her frame changed again but this time to one he had been accustomed to seeing. The curvy milf form that she loved to the sport. He didn't understand why, but then, he never really took the opportunity before to ask her why she preferred the form.

Hands began roaming across her breasts. She cooed a bit and licked her lips. He got the drift of her message.

"I'm a little, worshipped out," he said to Aurora with an emphasis on the out. It wasn't as if he wouldn't want more. Even if he didn't Aurora had gotten especially well-versed in persuading him.

"Fine, but bothers me how stressed you are already."

"Look at this," he said with a wave of his arm.

"At what? A few clothes and wet spots easily dealt with?"

Now that he looked at the mess it looked much smaller than before.

"Still, you don't know how my dad will react to anything," he said while a wave of fear washed over him. Her eyes went red. "He may even hate what I did here."

"Your father doesn't scare me."

"No," he said with a laugh. "I'd imagine not."

He moved through the living room picking up discarded clothes. Meredith's were the weirdest for him is that the cops' uniforms fabric felt stiff in his hands. The body armor, heavy with alien weight, strained his arms as he moved it to hide it in a closet.

After picking it up, he surveyed the wets spots and his eyes wandered over to Aurora once again.

"You can have me again if you want?" she said sitting up. Brushing her hair aside her pink eyes bore into him.

"You're insatiable," he told her, but within seconds, his cock sprang up.

"Don't project your own lusts onto me," she said with a laugh. "Besides, I can take care of myself if needed right now."

Jacob saw the challenge in her eyes. The daring of him to the walkway.

"You slut," he said with a growl.

"Take me," she giggled.

Within seconds, her legs were wrapped around his waist as he thrust into her. He would grunt, and she gasped into his ear. Jacob felt a surge of power within himself as her thrust into her. As if the depths of her couldn't be reached.

Aurora for her part didn't seem keen on holding back herself. Yells and gratuitous moans filled the air. And so did the sopping sounds of pussy being pounded.

It didn't take long for Aurora to erupt into an orgasm. Heralded by her sudden stiffening and nails digging into his back. He yelped, not registering the spray of fluid hosing him. She didn't let off as he thrust away, trying himself to reach the end.

He came. And thankfully too. With a grunt, he replenished the fluids she lost. And he knew that his spurting flood of cum into her would. Nothing about bodily fluids escaped her, especially cum. Something she made known to him during their first encounters. Exhausted, he relaxed on top of her, breathing heavily while she cooed.

"I could never imagine how humans got this lucky," she said. Long breaths could be heard going in as Jacob laid his head on her breast.

"I think I love you," he said with a content sigh.

"Master," Aurora spoke with a tender voice. "I am honored by such a declaration. Know that none will ever have a place in my heart as you."

"Will you sleep with other men?"

"The will of the Goddess imposes many things, but as I know with you humans, it is in direct issue with the idea of a relationship. Plus you do own me in many ways."

Jacob thought for a moment.

"I guess it would be hard to impose on you with a cock that needs to be dipped in everything to worship the goddess properly."

"Precisely," she said with a sudden exhale of air. "And anyway, I could never really wander away from you. If anything, we can think of ourselves in an open relationship."

"That is new, but what if I find someone I like?"

"Concubines are fine with me as long as we share them."

"You mean men?"

She let out a laugh.

"You don't think some group sex like we had tonight would be out of the norm?"

Jacob never even considered the possibility of a double-dipping scenario. While two clams in the sea were fine to one eager sausage. Having two sausages competing for one clam struck him as a queer idea. But with the whims of lusts, Aurora would obey the Goddess's commands and so would he.

"Can we keep it rare though?" he asked.

Aurora laughed.

"We are but covetous vessels after all," she said through deep breaths.

"Your heartbeat is calming," Jacob finally said after a minute of silence. Listing to its beat lulled him into sleep and soon he found himself back in the darkness of his dreams.

Jacob had grown accustomed to dreaming about the throne. A chair is centered atop a set of stonework with intricate designs carved into the surface. It honestly looked like a step pyramid with stairs leading up to the chair. The floor of the place also felt rough on the bare bottoms of his feet. Only in the circle of light around the entire thing could he see that the floor's surface was a black stone.

The throne area is where he first met Aurora weeks ago in his dream. After her larval state attached to his cock. Here she had proposed the sexual arrangements with him to give herself a physical form. A form tied to his own now.

Jacob, as every night he dreamt now, avoided the throne. Aurora never seemed to be present in this dream world now or at least in the light. So for the past few nights, he ventured away from the throne and into the darkness.

Now, the first time Jacob did this unprescribed adventure, the argument of how dangerous any deviation from the light raged on inside him.

Eventually, he decided to step away, and thus far he knew that if he went right, eventually the stone turned to dirt. Left yielded water. Behind the structure of the throne and it seemed as if the stone kept going. Tonight, he would journey by immediately turning around and walking.

Into the darkness, which quickly light from the throne didn't carry on far. He got the distinct impression this structure represented some sort of haven in these outlying dark lands. If there existed one though, why couldn't there be another?

Forging on, Jacob walked and walked. Nothing permeated the darkness. Not even the changing of what he walked on. Logically if the stonework didn't end, then a road must be underfoot. Under that impression, he walked until he walked into something hard.

The object he ran into smacked him hard in the face. Reaching out, he felt a stone wall and he moved down its length, fingers finding the seams of mortar holding the bricks together. As he did, he eventually found a corner and turned it. As soon as he had, a chant began.

The language sounded alien. Ignoring its insistent words, he moved along the wall until another corner. He rounded it. When he did, the chanting ceased. The silence and darkness re-permeated the air once again. The only thing that broke the spell beside his breath, and a little red light sat insignificantly a few feet away. Sensing no danger, Jacob moved away from the safety of the wall and to the light.

As Jacob got closer, a cold shiver ran up his spine. Power permeated the air. As he moved up to the light, he felt a push back against him. Ignoring it, he moved up quickly to snatch the gem.

Pain.

The suddenness of it brought him to his knees.

'Who are you," a voice deep as the darkness spoke.

Jacob struggled under the power of the thing.

"I ask the same," Jacob said, struggling to say the words through clenched teeth.

"I am Kloth," it said. "A ruler in this realm.'

"This is a dream," Jacob said. He felt himself growing numb to the pain a bit.

"A mortal then," it said with a hiss. "To whom do you serve?"

"There is no name," he said clenching his teeth. His voice came out like a hiss. "Just a feeling."

Silence.

Jacob took a moment to look at the gem. Red and hard like the stone itself, but power within.

"I have no recollection of which of us ancients have been awoken," the deep voice spoke. "But you have awoken a second now."

"And what does that mean?"

"It means that I will have to find a champion for myself to use now."

"And what will they champion?"

"They will champion me, the bringer of sorrowful desires." 'What does that even mean?" he asked with a laugh.

'You dare laugh at me mortal?

Another searing pain went through him. With that, Jacob woke with a start. Absolutely fearful of the dream now that he had escaped back to reality. Here, he also awoke somewhere else. In his bed, Jacob ripped the blankets back.

"What's going on?"

Aurora sat up as Jacob scrambled out of the bed.

"It's a real place isn't it?"

"What is?" Aurora said with a stretch.

"The place I first met you, in my dreams."

Aurora looked at him, her eyes yellow. A color he hadn't seen before.

"Why do you ask now?"

"Ever since that night, I dream about it."

She was silent as her eyes shifted to blue.

"You still dream of that place?"

"Yeah," he said walking over and sitting in his office chair. "Who is Kloth?"

Aurora's eyes shifted to yellow again.

You can interact there?

'Yeah," he replied. "And why is the throne the only place with light?

Eyes deepened even more into yellow.

"No entity in that place has a name," she said. "You gave me mine."

Jacob was about to respond when her eyes flared into the red.

"You walked around?" she said angrily with a snarl.

"When I asked about it you said nothing to worry about."

"I didn't think you could walk around in it," she said. Her eyes faded from red to blue suddenly. "No matter, where that is, something has to have a physical form to come here. You gave me that and you need to understand how dangerous other beings from there can be."

"You didn't warn me and now another named one is awakened?"

"One with a name, you gave me mine."

She shifted in the bed, the sheets rustling with the movement. Swearing to himself that he could feel her heat from here and he locked eyes with her. They were pink now and she licked her lips.

"We don't have time to have sex," he replied.

"I don't think you get it. Worship isn't an option."

"I get it, but I worry about my dad, who may not react well to anything going on." "You worry too much," she said with a stretch, her form changing to match a woman closer to his age. His dad would have an issue with how milfy she would look. Now the exaggerated curves were gone. She took a petite look and was a bit smaller than him.

"With everything shrunk, how are you an emissary for the goddess?"

Aurora stood up, her petite body barely sinking into the bed. He saw that her ginormous breasts were now close to a b-cup. That would be the extent that he got to see as she jumped down from the bed and sauntered over to him.

Aurora hated body hair. Something he noticed every time seeing her naked. Now that he thought about it, he wondered if she would grow hair out or not. He had no basis on really if she did like hair or not. She just never did. Suddenly she was in his lap, eyes completely pink now.

"It's time for the morning sermon and we haven't done it before in your office chair."

Aurora looked predatory locking eyes with him. A tongue licked across the lips.

"Praise the goddess for this meal," she said hotly into his ear. No need to even work him up. Hard already and a shift from her, the length slid into her tight depths. "I always like taking you to the hilt."

"Yeah, but what if my dad comes home?"

"And hears the screams of his son railing a girl into submission?" she said.

"Wouldn't it be you riding me into submission?"

"Oh Jacob," she moaned. "I don't plan on riding you right now, you need more practice."

Oh.

"Yeah," she started and then began a passionate kiss, entwining her tongue with his as it swirled around. By the time they broke, Jacob became aware of how much he now needed some friction between their sexes. By now, her desires ran abundantly.

"I see what you did," he said.

"Do you?"

A mischievous challenge in her words and a slight grin on her face.

"All you have to do is take it."

"Can't take something freely give."

"But you can fuck it."

"Fuck it?"

"Yes."

The conviction in his mending soul came out. Punctuated by a surge of strength. He lifted his petite eldritch slut up. Turned her a bit, threw a leg over his shoulder, and proceeded to ram home with all his might. What astounded him at the moment is how easily the holding her up.

"Jacob, harder," she cried out, further astounding him was her push back of meeting his thrusts. Something about it seemed like he got deeper into her lithe body than ever before.

Can you feel me in your throat?

"Almost," she groaned out, nails digging into his shoulder as she twisted a bit. "To get that I need more leverage."

And Aurora lived up to the statement. Meeting his thrust even harder now and he swore he slid even deeper in. No matter, soon they both fell to the floor, each of them sputtering out their respective orgasmic fluids.

"How are we gonna clean this up," he said with heavy breaths as sweat stung his eyes. "You worry too much," Aurora sighed.

"Probably smells like sex."

"And what will that matter?"

"My father may not react well."

"To his son getting laid?"

Jacob shifted and stood up.

"Especially being that he has called me queer on more than a few occasions."

"Love is love," she said with a stretch. "Doesn't matter with who or how. Seems to me your species would struggle in general finding ones to love with as many hang-ups present."

"I'm pretty open."

"You aren't who I refer to," she replied pointing at him. "All of the women so far who have joined our conclave of sex fiends have all been difficult to convince. All of them had hang-ups about the process and after. Though by now, the teacher will emerge soon, the cop will cocoon shortly and our office assistant, well is enjoying herself immensely."

"You can tell?"

"There's a telepathic link."

A moment of silence as Jacob digested the information. Something was meant by her statement. Possibly a warning of sorts. Then again, Aurora may have wanted him to know these things. He wouldn't ask for clarification.

"I need a shower."

And Jacob left Aurora in the room, naked on the floor. Though to him, she seemed to be sunning her lithe body. He tried not to think about it as he showered. Any twitch of his cock would no doubt summon forth Aurora. That thought made him smile as he soaped up.

"How can I be so dedicated to self-control now?" he asked himself out loud. Though he did know. Everything had changed for him. There wasn't a persistent hunger anymore.

"When did I eat last?"

Getting out of the shower, he couldn't actually recall his last meal. His stomach didn't growl to agree with it and he wondered briefly why. As he dried off, Aurora came into the bathroom, still naked.

"Showering?"

And drinking.

He watched as she turned the sink on and leaned in to drink from the faucet. Thinking the way she drank from the sink faucet was weird, he wanted to comment that a tentacle mouth would work better.

Holding a hand up, he went to correct her of the action, but one look of her fat pussy lips from behind stopped him. Instantly hard and unable to now look away, he did the one thing that he could.

Aurora coughed heavily as he slid himself into her. Leaving her no chance, Jacob moved in and out of her without restraint. Eventually, he grabbed her hair and yanked her head up, careful that he didn't hurt her.

Her coughs tightened her pussy around his cock. Not that he cared, but he went at it even as she pushed her back against his chest.

"Fuck," Aurora yelled. She tensed and then began shaking as if she was having a seizure. Jacob felt a bit disappointed that Aurora didn't hold off her orgasm longer. Mostly because the flood of juices would over lubricate. Jacob didn't want to spend a lot of time with sex at the moment. That is until their thrusts were misaligned and he slid out of her pussy. On the next thrust, the tunnel he slid into wasn't her pussy anymore.

"Goddess damn it all."

"I'm sorry," Jacob said, panicking at the thought of hurting her. Grasping her cheeks, he spread them to try and ease pulling out of her. Much to his surprise, she pushed back hard and it caused him to lose his footing. Falling back, his back stopped against the wall. Aurora followed him the entire way. Still holding her cheeks apart, she shoved her petite self back, impaling his cock deep into her.

"Finally taking what you want," Aurora sighed at him. A hand reached up a pulled his head into her shoulder. Instinctively he bit into her neck, which caused her to shove back even more. "Stop holding back Jacob."

He looked forward, eyes locking with her solid pink ones in the mirror. Letting go of her neck, he licked his lips.

"Yes," she hissed, her own tongues coming out with a swirl of tentacled horror. At that moment, he remembered how alien the woman could be. With a smile, he reached down.

"Jump," he said.

She did. Not a big jump, he never left the inside of her as she did. He caught her legs and hoisted them up. Straining a bit as he did, it took a second to hold her so he could drive himself in and out of her ass. Concentrating on his hand at the task, which the difficulty of it made his arms strain, he barely saw the tentacles begin sprouting from her body.

At first, the tentacles started with her hair and she lost her composure. The second, and one he almost missed by closing his eyes, is that her labia swelled and pulled apart like a flower blossoming. Tendril waved into the air from her sex. The sight almost caused him to drop her, but she reached back with both hands and wrapped them around the back of his head. Her eyes were closed, but her mouth was not.

"I'm not gonna hold it," she said suddenly.

"Neither am I," Jacob grunted, shoving himself up and as deep into her ass as he could. The feeling of hot cum spurting out of the tip of his cock felt as if it were being pulled by a vacuum suddenly. His orgasm stretched out but while he tensed for the moments it happened, Aurora seemed to buck hard against him. Finally, the orgasm subsided and he let Aurora sink to the floor. And sink she did, his deflating cock came out of the ring of her ass with an audible popping sound.

"Fuck," he said, trying to maintain his stance. Everything burned in his arms and legs. Looking at himself in the mirror, it seemed to him that he looked a bit skinnier. His stomach rumbled in reply. "What did you do?"

I took what you gave willingly," she said with a heavy sigh. "That was some thick cum.

"Shouldn't that be a bad sign?"

"Why? It's perfectly normal for a man of your age to produce load after a load of thick spunk. It's tasty and I am always going to enjoy absorbing it."

"You're weird," he said with a laugh. Noting that she could have used any other way of describing her consumption of cum. "I'm gonna dress and get some food. You should shower."

Jacob left her in the bathroom laying naked on the floor.

Minutes later, Jacob found himself in the kitchen, worried about what to make to eat. There didn't happen to be anything to make. With a sigh, he decided to order something. What Jacob didn't want was to leave and have his father show up. Man would be liable to do something. Though, as he would find, in short order Aurora's plans differed.

"Let's go out," she said walking into the kitchen.

Jacob looked at her in surprise.

"And don't start with your dad," she said pointing at him. Aurora wore the nubile petite form.

"Where did you get clothes to fit?"

"I watched some stuff on hemming. Made my own," she replied. "And don't change the subject. I know we have no food in the house because I ate it all. Won't you worry if your dad comes home to that?"

Damn, you're right," Jacob replied.

"So, let's go out."

"We don't have a car, I had to steal a shopping cart the last time."

"Do you even have a license?"

"I do," he said pulling it out of his wallet and holding it up to her for inspection.

"We need to get this retaken, it doesn't flatter you at all."

She gave him the plastic back. This moment marked the first time she had said something negative about how he looked before they met.

"Don't look at me like that," she said, her eyes turning blue. She walked up to him and pulled him into a kiss.

"I'm just saying that with how you look now, the picture doesn't match."

Jacob let it go. He had to. Aurora was the first woman to show him anything close to true friendship and companionship. A fear of his is that everything centered on the fake. He wanted to be truly loved and wanted. The alien seemed to be genuine to him.

"Alright," he said. "Should I call a cab?"

She nodded.

"Let's get food first."

And that is how Jacob went out for the first time on a date with Aurora. Within the hour, she was next to him, sitting in a booth at a dimly lit sushi restaurant. Everything was going great as Aurora devoured everything she could on the menu. The Waitress had been more than astounded with the amounts.

"Are you sure we can afford this?" Aurora asked putting down the last of the previous plate.

"Yeah, but with your small form, you may want to slow down."

She sighed.

"It's so good, but you are right. If I keep it up, my metabolism will slow and I will have to start storing the energy."

"So after we pay, store?"

"Figured we need a car," she said with a smile. She drank a glass of water, down in a few gulps.

"You just want me to buy a car?"

"Yeah, why not?" she said as a matter of fact. "You need one and you can afford one."

Bu-

"And your father won't care, I promise." "Why wouldn't he?"

He'll be distracted.

Sated for now of the fear of the patriarch, Jacob sat back in the booth thinking. He had no idea what kind of car to buy. The thought of ever buying one at his previous size would never fly. Feeling excited by the prospect, he decided it would be a great idea.

"Okay," he said. "I need to pay the bill."

"I can just offer myself up," she said with a laugh. "Though, it would mean being out later."

"Relax, I feel the need too, but we can't in such a public place."

"And you're in no rush to see me experiment with other men yet."

"My cock seems to be filling you up just nicely."

The waitress walked up, blushing heavily as the conversations turn in the direction that was overheard. She gave the bill quickly and walked off.

"She's cute," Aurora said.

"You think so?"

"Yeah and horny. You can practically smell the lust on her."

Interest peeked, Jacob looked around and watched the Asian girl as she moved through the restaurant. A petite Asian girl who looks adorable in her black pants suit. He did forget the establishment prided itself on a professional appearance.

She eventually walked back up, returning his stare as she did. The girl couldn't stammer out much, but by the end of the exchange, they paid and the girl had his number.

I can't believe you," Jacob said to her as they walked out the door.

"What? We need recruits."

He sighed knowing how right she was. Not to mention, their circle of cultists needed to grow more to survive. With another sigh, he let her lead the way out. Minutes later, they were at a dealership.

Now, Jacob wanted something utility-like in its inception. His whole reason was having a moving shagging vehicle that could also transport groups fit a communal better. Aurora, while she did agree, insisted time was on their side and such things could wait. Jacob quickly found himself actually being pushed into buying something for himself.

"It's sweet of you to be so responsible, but take this moment not to be."

"Even if I do this, we will have to get it registered and I have no insurance."

She smiled and stopped him.

So far they had been walking away from the sushi restaurant and moving to a car dealership. Though the particular area had more than a few on the same strip. Suddenly, she was in his arms, kissing him passionately. A few cars honks later and they were back to walking. Even holding hands as they did.

Jacob never flashed cash anywhere. Even as a rule to anyone. Too many bullying events left him often with no money. Thankfully, he had cards to different accounts that he owned. Turns out, unless they could get him to take money off of them, which never happened, bullies didn't care for plastic. As they walked up to a dealership, that fact resonated with him as a dealer walked up to them.

"Hey folks," he said in greeting arms open in welcome. He wore a grey pressed suit and looked professional with his hair greased back. With black hair and a white smile, he welcomed them. "What can I help you with?"

"We're looking for a car," Aurora said with a giggle.

"Ah well is it for the lady?"

The two of them talked, leaving Jacob out of the conversation. So he looked out into the car yard and saw little that drew his interest. He automatically surmised that a bigger vehicle would do for him. In the end, he decided that the best vehicle to get was a small SUV.

Moments later, Jacob had returned to the two of them. He interrupted the man and informed him of the exact vehicle he wanted. The man didn't seem too happy that Jacob returned and thus began talking to Jacob.

The man prattled on about costs and the like. Jacob, who had experience with contracts found himself seeing something wrong. The number of fees and taxes seemed completely off. While Jacob felt his anger rising to the transgression, Aurora suddenly excused herself to use the restroom.

Fifteen minutes later, the contract negotiation didn't seem to be going well. The phone rang and the man excused himself, snatching the contract fast before walking out. Seconds later Aurora sat back next to him grinning ear to ear.

"What?" he asked her after a few seconds.

"I got a better deal for you," she said licking her fingers.

What did you do?

"We have our first male recruit, though he will need to be bonded to someone soon." "You didn't."

"I did and let me tell you, he was tasty for sure," she said with a laugh. "He is lucky to be the first male recruit."

"Oh," Luke said, a bit disappointed that Aurora couldn't contain herself. "Why did you do that?"

"The car will be cheaper and we can get out of here sooner."

Interrupting his retort and punctuating her point, the dealer walked up, scratching his head in confusion.

"Never seen this before," he spoke sitting down in front. Soon enough, money exchanged hands, to which the dealership balked at the cash purchase in full. They even tried to negotiate add-ons during the payment so that the contract could be amended for them. He knew the game and refused.

Sitting in the car, Jacob drove around with Aurora. She laughed uncontrollably throughout the ride. The laughter disturbed Jacob a bit as the unabated joy of another person took him into a weird place. He pulled over on a side road and stopped the vehicle in fear that something was wrong.

No sooner had the car stopped, than she launched into a tirade of how exciting riding in a car was. She laughed more and he joined in. Soon enough, she had pulled him into the back of the car. Minutes or even an hour later, Jacob did lose track of time sometimes trying to satiate Aurora's appetites. By the time they finished, Jacob worried his father would beat them home.

So in fear, they drove home. Aurora laughed once more, enjoying the thrill of the ride. As they pulled up, he thankfully saw that his father's car didn't sit in the drive. With a sigh of relief, they left without even stepping out of the vehicle.

"Where are we going?" Aurora asked with a moan.

The moan caught Jacob's attention. A quick look over and watched hands rubbing across nipples. One thing about Aurora is that she loved nipples. He figured that out as he often saw him touching them. With a smile, he looked back out to the road.

"Figure the grocery store."

"Oh."

Jacob stole a glance at her after her exclamation. What he saw was her shirt up and pert breasts out. Skirt up, she had pulled her legs up and had her mouth agape as her head lay back against the headrest. It didn't take more than a second to see that Aurora's fingers buried themselves into her snatch.

"Hey now on the new seats?" he asked with mock anger.

"But it's so wet," Aurora groaned. "And it feels so good."

"But the seats?"

Suddenly the windshield became covered in a sprayed mist as Aurora let out a scream. Jacob didn't stop the vehicle, but her scent overpowered the new car smell immediately.

"Fuck that was good," she said with a punctuated sigh. It drew his attention once more for a second and he saw her licking her fingers. Suddenly her head snapped his way. "Want a taste?"

He opened his mouth to respond and suddenly her salty cunt juiced fingers were shoved into his mouth. Without much of a choice, Jacob licked her fingers clean. While Aurora moaned her appreciation, she did make sure that each finger got sucked on properly. After that, she pulled her hand away.

"That turned me on even more," she said to him, biting her lip. "It's getting hard to stay in this conservative form."

"You only had to be in that form when my dad was around," Jacob said with a laugh before concentrating back on the road.

"I know, but it's nice to be more on your level with my size."

"Does it bother you to have curves?"

"No silly," she said laughing. "But it bothers me that my curves can be intimidating for others to see me have when I am with you."

"We haven't been out in public," Jacob replied trying to piece together when Aurora got the idea.

"The cop made a comment when she first saw me and it seemed fitting after you said something about your dad."

"I didn't mean to make you conservative with your form."

The car stopped as Jacob pulled into a parking spot at the grocery. Looking over at her, he saw that she wore a look of concern on her face as she returned his gaze.

"I love your curves, but I worried that with your motherly look and how affectionate you can be, it could draw unwanted attention." 'What do you mean?

"An older woman, curvy as you especially, would put out that you were my mother or worse, some sort of predator on younger males. With me still in high school, people could call the authorities."

"That makes sense," she said falling silent. Shifting around, he looked out the windshield while she fixed her clothes. Left a moment to his own thoughts, he almost laughed thinking how funny it was that he gave her a hard time about the affections of a milfy woman. The windows weren't tinted and here they were with her tits hanging out.

The car door opened and Aurora bounded out with a long stretch. Jacob smiled to himself, hoping that she would be alright. He couldn't imagine how hard it must be on her. How hard it must be on the others as well.

With a sigh, he got out of the car and hopped that Aurora didn't have any shenanigans for the shopping.

They went into the store, and Aurora wasted no time in filling a cart. Thankfully, her interest lay only in finding food at the moment. He guessed it had to do with a concentration on making sure whatever fuel food grabbed would work to facilitate worshipping.

Jacob balked at the foods chosen, many on the healthier side, and often wondered how easy it would be to fall back into old habits.

"Hey, so why all the healthy food?"

"Don't need all the junk food," she replied. "I worry how hard it will be to maintain my own mass if I eat the greasy food all the time. Plus, I need healthier options for my tastes."

Jacob didn't say anything about her mindset. In all actuality, he worried about the vulgarity of her bathroom practices if he asked. No doubt inappropriate not only in public but in her privacy.

Eventually, the shopping ended. They checked out and after two hours, they were back on the road.

"That was fun," Aurora said with a laugh.

"Yeah, but it's a lot."

Jacob stole a glance at the back seat. Not only did the groceries fill the trunk up, but also the entirety of the backseat. He worried for a moment that the amount wouldn't fit at home. They pulled up and Jacob let out a sigh of relief that his father's car still wasn't there.

"It's about time for dinner," Aurora said.

"Yeah?"

"Bring the groceries in, I would like to cook for you."

And she was gone. Jacob felt a queer feeling in the pit of his stomach. Not one of fear, but a rising excitement that he didn't understand. Normally, any such commands from his father would have scurried him into action. But by Aurora's command, he needed to fulfill not only because he didn't fear her, but he genuinely wanted to please her. With a smile, he did as she bid.

It took Jacob almost twenty minutes to bring in all the groceries. Aurora moved much quicker than he thought possible when it came to putting them up. Before long, he stood in awe while watching her lithe body as she filled cabinet space. Aurora even organized by types of food and soon, everything looked to be in a proper place.

"All done," she said with a laugh.

"What's all done?"

The deep voice cut the atmosphere like a knife. Jacob turned slowly and walking into the kitchen was his father. There was malice about him as he stepped in. Then he stopped at the doorway.

Jacob looked at his suit-wearing father and saw the malice burning in the man's eyes.

His gaze swept over the kitchen. Not looking at Aurora, he was surprised when she walked up to him and hugged him from the side.

"Jacob is this your father?"

The patriarch looked slowly from Aurora to him.

"You're not Jacob."

"Yeah dad, I am."

There, he saw the fist clench around the clasp of the suitcase. It relaxed and the suitcase leaned up soon on the wall. A queer look passed over the man's face but he looked over to Aurora.

"Who is this then?"

And like that, his father fell into an act that Jacob found astounding. As hours passed, Aurora and his father chatted while they ate the prepared meal. Jacob's father had many stories to share and honestly, Jacob felt jealous of the attention she showed him with her open-ended questions. Time went and Jacob watched the clock until it hit about eight. Not included much in the conversation, he began to doze off a bit. Until that is when a knock on the door.

"I'll get it," Jacob said thankfully to bound out of the dining room. Moving through the house, the knocks urged him to be quicker, Jacob opened the door, half expecting to see a cop looking for Meridith.

Instead, standing in front of him was a goddess of absolute beauty. Ms. Devons had an aura of sexuality that wafted off her like an over pheromones french whore. With a modest dress of blue jeans and a red blouse. Her dark hair was cropped and she wore glasses that gave off a librarian vibe.

His cock responded in kind to her look, springing uncomfortably in his pants and straining against the fabric. Memories of fucking her whorish holes at the school while she begged for more of his cock made him struggle. No doubt he would step outside and take her without any complaint from her.

"You need to play along," she said with a smile.

"Okay."

"Jacob, who is it?"

His dad's harsh voice went through the house. It almost made him wince. Thankfully the perceived threat of his father wouldn't be picked up by anyone but him. No one experienced his father's wrath but him. Locking eyes with Ms. Devons, he knew he wore a look of worry on his face.

"Tell him the truth," Ms. Devons said.

It's my English teacher, Ms. Devons," he called over his shoulder.

Is that your father?

"Yeah," he replied "What does she want?"

His father's gruff voice cut again into the air. He saw a grimace pass across Ms. Devons' face. But then she winked at him.

"Won't be too bad I hope," she said before brushing past him. "Mr. Grand."

Jacob stood with the door open still, flabbergasted with his teacher showing up. After a minute, he closed the door and went to sit in the living room. A few moments later, Aurora joined his living room.

"That's going well," she said with a smirk.

"Is that what you meant by distraction?"

"Yep."

Aurora's legs kicked out from her as she swung the in repetition. Jacob thought it made her look like a teenager on a swing. The look gave her an erotic innocence, but he knew that to be false.

"My father do anything to you?"

"I could tell he was attracted, but it's one line I wouldn't cross on you."

That implication made him feel better a bit about the situation. Not a good thing if his father aggressively went for Aurora. Whatever hope that his father's safety would be thrown away at that point. Even Aurora's sexual persuasions wouldn't keep him in agreement with her if that happened.

"And besides," she said leaning towards him on the couch and grabbing his cock. "I can tell you I prefer the buck and bull you have to his verminous ways."

He smiled, feeling the tension slip away for anticipation.

"Ms. Devons changed fast."

"She hasn't been completed yet."

A hand on his face pulled his gaze to hers.

"Make no mistake, your father wouldn't survive an encounter with any of my kind under normal circumstances."

"Not because of me?"

"Not, he was deemed unworthy by touch. But you're important and so making an exception, for now, isn't a big deal."

"When does it end?"

"Whenever you say or when he pursues the sun."

The invocation of Icarus took him aback.

"You've been watching t.v.?"

"No," she said with a laugh. "I didn't like the commercials so I swapped to looking at the computer."

She pulled back with a sigh.

"I didn't plan for your father all that much.'

"What do you mean?"

"I can't stay here can I?"

"Oh yeah, we didn't address that issue."

Jacob didn't even think of Aurora as being able to stay with him that night or any night while his dad occupied the house.

"I could have bought you a place today."

"It's okay," she said with a laugh. "I can go to Ms. Devons for the night while we work a more permanent solution out."

"Should I take you home?"

A quizzical look passed on her face.

"Doesn't Ms. Devons need some time with my dad and don't we need some time." Aurora smiled big at the hint.

"Hey dad, I'm gonna take Aurora home."

There was a giggle and then a muffled reply. With a shrug, Jacob stood up from the couch and reached back for Aurora.

Shall I, my lady?

"Such a gentleman."

He pulled her up and she followed his lead. Outside, after the door closed, Jacob pulled Aurora into an embrace. Head buried into her shoulder she took a deep breath. Nothing smelled so sweet in the world to him than the flowery scent of her. After a few moments, he let the embrace go.

"So do you know where she lives?" Jacob asked as he turned away, wiping his face with his arm.

"Of course," Aurora replied as she skipped up to him. Soon enough they were driving along the road to the house.

Minutes passed with nothing being said between them.

"You know," Jacob said after they stopped at a light. "I always wanted to be the kid in the back seat looking up at my parent in bewilderment at them. Curious of how such a love could exist and create such a happy family."

Aurora was silent.

"I can't imagine a day where that was true though."

"We could find a place and fuck in the back seat."

Jacob looked over at her. Aurora shrugged.

"Way I figure, we can talk about what it's like to have that view, or we can try to make it a reality."

He laughed. A hearty deep laugh and soon as the light turned, he sped through the streets looking for a place to make it a reality. Though, it didn't take long for a place to be found. Situated in some trees behind a park, they both went in the backseat as quickly as they could.

Jacob found that stripping the back seat while Aurora peppered him with kisses. Their lips met a lot, and eventually, she ripped the fabric of his boxers away.

"Hey," he said in protest of the action.

"Shut up and fuck me."

Sliding into her, she giggled when he bit her neck.

Jacob stared at the cocoon.

Secured to the wall, the greenish-brown pod pulsed with life. While smaller in size compared to Aurora's pod, it looked formidable all the same. With a bulbous body, it looked like a pregnant belly. Rebirth for service to the goddess. With a sigh, he sat down in front of the pod.

Inside the pod, Meredith changed. Meredith, a cop, found herself the day before as the latest inductee into the religion devoted to lust. Jacob didn't know why he sat there in front of the pod, but he currently had nowhere else to be.

Everything with Aurora over the past few days left him a bit overwhelmed and three days ago, he awoke to find her missing. With nothing left to do, meandered to Meredith's after a ton of research into where she lived. Thankfully, the internet provided the answer. That's why he sat here now, trying to breathe a bit. With his father being home and the lack of attention from Aurora, he felt overwhelmed.

School bored him now. Subjects that he once flocked to now meant little to him because his cock throbbed almost constantly looking for something to sink into. Honestly, he kept himself at bay, but today he skipped as his balls hurt painfully now. Three days and he hadn't seen Aurora since he dropped her off at Ms. Devons. He tried not to be upset about it, but after three days, he felt abandoned.

Jacob hadn't tried to go to Ms. Devons after being there once. A seen student would cause issues. Now that he thought about that issue as all that important, getting discovered outweighed any physical need he had. Even now, staring at the pod, his cock throbbed in sick determination.

"I fucked the pod Aurora was in," he said. "Would there be any different here?"

Standing up, he groaned in frustration. By now his pants sat at his ankles. Looking at the angry head of his snake spurting out thick globs of white pre-cum. His gaze slowly fell onto the bulbous pregnant-looking sac.

The black tendrils moved tentatively across the surfaces of the room. As he studied the pod and its body, he got a distinct feeling what he was about to do, would be welcome. The pod made no move towards him as he stepped up to it. Placing a hand on its brown surface, he marveled a bit.

The sac felt warm under the touch. A beat pulsed through it. Even leaning up and pressing an ear to it, he thought he could even hear rhythmic breathing. So much about it made no sense to him.

"What happens in there?" he asked in a whisper. "Does it hurt when the change happens? Does one turn into a soup?"

Jacob felt ridiculous asking the questions. Aurora kept a lot from him concerning the workings of her alien physical traits. That or she didn't know herself and that possibility made Jacob more curious than anything. Surmising the priestess probably cared only about knowledge dealing with lustful-oriented things. Biology wouldn't matter to her, but then, Jacob did think the high school's biology teacher would be interested.

"Ms. Brooks definitely would like this," he said with a mischievous smile. "Wonder how she would feel about cross-breeding."

Holding his cock, he presses against the warm skin of the sac. Feeling the warmth caused a shiver of pleasure to run into his toes. Then, not knowing what else to do, he pushed his cock against the membrane of the sac.

Jacob got the impression quickly that the sac membrane mimicked latex in its response. While he could slide his cock to be surrounded by the body of the sac. Though, try as he might, the friction did not feel good on his cock. Deflated with the defeat, he prepared to pull away.

"What-?"

A powerful force gripped his cock. Then, a warmth surrounded his phallus that spread quickly throughout his whole body.

"Who's there?"

The voice was female.

"Meredith?"

"Yes."

It's me, Jacob.

Hey Jacob," she replied. Her voice sounded happy.

"How are you talking?"

"I'm still in the cocoon then?" she replied. "It takes a while for the change to happen." "Why?"

"The mind has to be preserved while the body is regrown."

Jacob was silent as he digested that information.

"Why are you here Jacob?"

"I have nowhere else to go right now and I am too horny to concentrate."

"How did you get in?"

"You left the back door unlocked."

"That makes sense," she said. "I was rushing to get inside before the physical changes began."

"Does it hurt?" he asked after a moment of silence.

"Best fucking orgasm I have ever had in my life," she said. Her words had conviction in them. "The explosion of light heralded the change."

"So it doesn't hurt now?"

The only thing that hurts is how patient I have to be for it to finish.

She was silent and a pull began in earnest on his cock. It felt nice.

"What are you impatient for?"

"Sex mostly, but moreover I now have been given a way to clean up the streets."

Jacob closed his eyes once more and allowed himself to enjoy the sensations.

"You can have the sex you know?"

"There isn't anyone."

"Well, like me, you need to find her. There are plenty of women who would thrive on this gift that you offer."

He didn't reply. The sucking around his cock became intense.

"Even now as you use me to please yourself, that backed-up baby batter is potent enough to force a change immediately in a woman."

Stars. He saw stars as his cock spurted shot after shot.

"That's it, feed me, Jacob. You're gonna make me a powerful flower when I bloom."

He didn't hear much. The stars danced and brought him into euphoria. As he washed in it, a tentacle slapped against him, sending him flailing onto the ground.

"What the hell?"

The cocoon hissed at him. Backing away, he didn't even realize that he had stood up. Tendrils danced from the side and Jacob understood that his welcome had been worn out.

Getting up, he shuffled away quickly. Tears rolled down his face.

"I'm so disgusting and worthless," he told himself as he left Meredith's room. "Even Aurora has abandoned me."

Jacob moved through the house, bumping into corners as he moved awkwardly. By the time he reached the stairs to go down them, he forced himself to stop.

"Fuck this," he said, fixing his clothes before starting down the stairs. "Everything was going great until my dad showed up. Think that prick even knows I'm the reason he is still alive? No. Mother fucker couldn't even believe that I can do anything."

Jacob mumbled to himself, trailing off as he exited the house. His vehicle sat there and roared to life as he drove away. Meredith's house quickly disappeared behind him as he left. As he drove through the urban streets, he thought about what she said.

He didn't know why the thought of finding an actual woman to fuck didn't cross his mind before. Every woman thus far approached him for sex. Would approaching a girl work for him? He thought about this and wondered briefly who would fit his tastes.

He already heard Aurora's thoughts on the matter as he thought this way.

"It's not about looks. Those will come with the change. It's about who is worthy to join us. Not all women are and by far not all men. But anyone who can serve the goddess will in their way."

There, of course, didn't exist a way to reply. Even though he knew Aurora and him could communicate telepathically, she hadn't used the ability with him since before she had a humanoid form. With a sigh, he decided going home didn't have any appeal.

Driving on the highway, Jacob felt relaxed. The road, even with traffic, felt freeing to him. Even as he sped, never going over the speed limit, his thoughts on everything meant nothing mattered about him to anyone in the world right now. Driven now, he drove for an hour to the next town thinking there would be meaning there somewhere.

Jacob parked the car near downtown and began walking the streets. The weather, sunny and bright, made him realize that a black shirt and jeans didn't reflect a good decision for the heat. Sweat accumulated uncomfortably in his pits.

"Probably should have taken a shower," he said to himself imagining how he smelt horrible to those around him. His walking pace slowed as he remembered the teasing from not even two months before. The bad smell clung to him before. Often described as rotting pig sweat, he gagged at the memory. Shuffling off the walk and into a diner, he almost ran into a short blonde.

"Slow down there hun," she said with a laugh.

"I'm sorry," he blurted out, looking around in almost a panic.

"It's fine hun," she said regaining his attention. The older blonde, a shorter woman by almost two heads to Jacob, looked up at him with a fake smile. They always were before and Jacob didn't like this was any different. "Do you want a seat?"

"Sure," he said replying to her and looking through the diner. No other customer sat in the place. The diner reflected the same as workers too. "Just you?"

"Naw hun," she told him grabbing a menu and beckoning him to follow.

Jacob stared at her backside as she walked. A light blue waitress uniform with a pink ascot and white apron gave him the impression of a pinup-type woman. In all actuality, as Jacob watched her hips swayed with her gait.

"Well?" she stopped suddenly and turned to look back at him.

Jacob smiled, but he didn't feel any heat rise in him at being caught. Moving forward, she led him to a booth in an almost obscure area.

"Pretty far huh?"

"Closer to the kitchen," she replied as he took a seat. The leather protested as he did.

"I'm the only one in as the owner at the moment. Afternoons during the weeks are slow," she stated with that smile before placing a menu in front of him. "Start you off with a drink?"

"Water please."

"Take a minute to look over the menu, I'll be back in a few."

And she left him sitting there. From her departure, he smelt the stench of stale cigarette smoke. No longer around, Jacob smiled thinking of an old saying.

"If she smokes, she pokes," he said under his breath. Relaxing, he looked around the diner and saw nothing. Old pictures in black and white. Low ambient lighting that wouldn't shine through the dark wood blinds, which hung over huge windows. Other than the shiny chrome trim on the edges of the wooden and blue surface, nothing else drew his attention. The ambiance reflected peace, and Jacob let out a content sigh.

Seconds or minutes may have passed while he leaned back into the cushion of the booth. A lull quickly fell over him and he may have dozed off. The next thing recalled startled him as the noise of glass thudded onto the table.

"Sorry bout that," the waitress said.

"Tea?" Jacob asked a little confused.

"Sweet tea hon," she said with a smile. Her teeth were inexplicably white and shiny. "My specialty and at this time, I don't get many who sample my tea."

She slightly bit her lip. There was an innuendo present that he didn't fully understand himself, but he thought the implication for the tea centered on womanly bits. Not wanting to be rude, even though water would have sufficed, and picked the glass up. With a tentative sip, he could sing to the heavens in praise of the sweet tea. The golden brown liquid danced down his throat in sugary sweetness. Before anyone blinked, he sat the glass down drained of the liquid where ice cubes swirled around.

"Wow," he complimented looking up at her. "Whatever you want to bring me I'll take."

She smiled at him. Hand reaching out, she grasped his hand.

"I hope you know, I have the best cooking experience here," she told him, locking eyes with his and the smile turning into a blank expression. He got the feeling that a serious persona took over her. Then again, he also noticed while she squeezed his hand, so soft it was her skin.

"Whatever you deem necessary, I will eat."

She smiled again and then let his hand go.

Let me get you more tea and I'll cook you something right up.

The waitress left him, only to return in a few seconds and top his drink off. Then she left again, disappearing into the back. Jacob took a deep breath, waiting for the food.

Minutes passed. No music kept him company and while he did have a phone, Jacob found the content in waiting. His thoughts wandered on this place and eventually he had an idea of the place. The waitress touched him. He knew that it wouldn't take long for her to succumb to whatever otherworldly influence he offered.

"I wonder if I can push it," he said out loud. His cock throbbed in agreement. With a shrug, he looked at the glass.

"Maybe I should wait for the food though," he commented, noting that sexual need could wait for a fuel up. Way women were when the change began, they tended to want for a lot of exertion. Sitting back, he took a breath, stowing himself.

In what seemed like an eternity for Jacob, he finally heard the sound of approaching steps. Moments later, a hot plate of fries and a burger sat before him.

"Make the best burger in town hun, eat up."

"Thank you," Jacob replied, but she already turned to leave. It left him wondering if there was a reason for her sudden change. Before she seemed more than happy to communicate. Now she left hurriedly without a word.

With a shrug, he ate the burger and fries. The whole thing tasted wonderful and after a bit, he sat back satisfied with the meal. Draining the iced tea glass, he let the cup make a hollow sound on the table, causing the ice cubes to shift about. As if summoning her, the waitress returned.

How was it?

"The best burger I have ever had," he told her. She smiled at him, but he could tell something was off with her now.

"Would you like dessert?"

"Do you have pie?"

Her face slightly reddened, and Jacob knew that the influence of whatever hit women when touching him worked. He almost felt bad, but then as she walked away after giving him an affirmative, that melted away. Jacob wanted to get off and this waitress would be the means for that.

Moments later, she returned placing a small plate with a slice of apple pie on it.

"You don't have cherry?" He asked looking up at her.

"I uh hun," she stammered out. Jacob knew then that she was ripe for the taking.

"I could use some hot and moist cherry pie."

If the waitress could turn even redder, Jacob would have sworn something was wrong with her. He pushed the pie aside.

"So cherry?"

"I have this?"

And to Jacob's delight, she lifted her skirt up.

"And that looks cherry," Jacob said with a smile looking at the red plump lips of a woman definitely in heat.

"I'm not sure," she replied, her word having pauses between each. He could see her inner thighs rubbing together, hiding her sex a bit. The scent of her need filled the air.

"Just climb on the table," Jacob demanded.

"Okay."

The waitress climbed into the booth seat across from Jacob. She sat on the table and swung herself around. Legs spread apart and he saw that she used the headrest of the booth behind her to steady herself. Taking a deep breath, he leaned in to savor her lewd scent.

"Not worried about other customers?"

She didn't say anything. Instead, a hand reached to her sex and spread the wet lips apart. Meat lips pulled apart, assaulting his nostrils with a pungent smell of desire. Without further hesitation, he leaned into her heat.

Warm wetness engulfed his cheeks as pussy lips slid across his face. Without any more chiding, he began licking pussy for all it was worth, using his tongue to lap up the salty-tasting fluids. He almost stopped after a moment to look up at her, but then her body finally shuddered after his tongue roamed through the valley of her sex.

"Ah fuck," she cried out. "It's been so long. Lick that pussy, honey."

Jacob felt all too happy to oblige the demand. While with sex, something he found fascinatingly amazing about women is how sensitive they could be.

Lick it, harder.

Suddenly nails dug into his skull, but he didn't mind the pain they brought. What he did mind over the minutes of lapping at the waitress's pussy, is that she began moving her hips to rub her pussy up and down his face. Of course, his tongue didn't stop. And neither did her growing foulness.

"Shit," she cried. "My pussy needs more, drink its filth."

Jacob would have found it comical, but she meant it. Suddenly, his face saturated under a deluge of liquid. He tried to pull away, but nails dug in harder as the waitress's piercing wail filled the air. Eventually, her grip weakened and he sat back in the chair and marveled at how salty the taste of her sat on his tongue.

"That was something," she said after a few moments. By the time the words left her mouth Jacob recovered.

"Not it wasn't," he said stepping out of the booth. The waitress watched him. In a flash, his hand reached out and grabbed an ankle. She let out a cry as he yanked her to the edge of the table. Standing in the aisle, his pants dropped down.

"That's huge," she with a look on her face that Jacob couldn't place. Still, look at the head of his cock, the swollen head resting on the bare flesh of her labia. Another thing he noted at the moment is how prevalent shaved pussy presented itself. Looking at the glistening pussy as its brown lips looked enticing.

"I'll lube it up."

He ran it a few times through her wet lips. Before long, he began pushing to get his cock into her. A few pushes were needed for her pussy to open and accept it. Even as the head of his cock slipped into her, he held back from a final push.

Ready?

He asked the question. Not only for her to brace herself now for the size, but also for what would come from the encounter. He knew the forces that worked between sex and Aurora. No doubt to Jacob now as he figured out a choice presented itself for the change. Once accepted, she would change like the others. Aurora offered no encouragement in the telepathic link to the idea. Until a differing opinion on the matter came forward, he would assume it was right.

He waited for her encouragement and locked eyes with her. After a minute, she nodded and Jacob felt a sense of relief wash over them.

They both moaned as he slid into her. Inches went in as he relished the feeling. An envelope of warmth and comfort around him as he went in. He hit the wall, but as he did, the waitress let out a throaty moan.

"I haven't been this filled before."

"I haven't filled you yet."

"No, you haven't," she replied, her body moving now in impatience. He shuddered with the feeling. "Get on with it."

The demand didn't surprise him, but the intensity of her words took him aback. As he locked eyes with her, he saw the lust in them in her gaze. With a smile, he then began rearranging her insides.

Each thrust was powerful. Jacob quickly built up a sweat under his efforts. He couldn't recall when he had yanked her off the table and bent her over it. All that mattered to him was the nice slapping sound their bodies made as he thrust into her.

Eventually, the waitress stopped making loud noises. Her voice had begun tapering off from the obscenities. Without much more effort from her, he surmised that he probably fucked her enough. After that thought, he relaxed and allowed himself to finish.

"Ah," he cried out as pump after pump of jizz shot into her. He saw stars as he did. A weight of stress and tension leaving his body. Maybe it went into her, a sort of offering to Aurora. That thought dissipated as his orgasm came to an end. Awash in post-coital bliss, Jacob pulled out and staggered back. Looking at the waitress, he saw the thick white cum flowing out slowly. The sight brought a smile to his face.

"That fills you up?"

She didn't answer. Jacob felt comical as he pulled two twenties out and placed them on the table next to her. He wondered briefly when the change would hit her. The thought of it made him worry being that the establishment had to have other workers at some point. Wandering to the front, he made sure his clothes were fixed before heading into the bathroom to wash his face.

The cold water felt nice on his face. He wasn't above walking around in triumph to the smell of pussy on his face, but he didn't want to attract unwanted attention from a passerby. The past people cringed as they passed due to the smell of him. Wiping his face off, he smiled at himself in the mirror before making sure everything was presentable about him. Then he left the restroom.

Walking out, he noticed that the waitress could no longer be seen from the front.

"Must have moved to the back," he said out loud to himself. He knew that if she moved that quickly to the back, she would probably be experiencing the change. It made him worry, but in another city, he shrugged with the knowledge that if something did get found out, nothing would be tied to him. With a smile, he moved to the door.

A push on the door and he almost slammed into it as it didn't yield. With surprise, he found that the door needed a button pushed to open. Laughing, he opened the door and made sure that it closed behind him. A pull on the handle and the door didn't budge. Off to the side, in a window hung a sign that said closed.

Jacob laughed again to himself. Nothing about the encounter made sense to him, but he got laid. Sex made him feel better and he almost skipped down the sidewalk to his car. He got in and started it up with a roar. Looking around, he didn't see anyone, but he didn't peel out of the spot and into the road.

Jacob drove back to his home feeling content with the day. Though he didn't start the day with any plan, he learned that he couldn't let life pass him by. There needed to be active on his part. Maybe that's why Aurora stayed silent for the time being.

He jumped when the ringing of his phone reverberated through the car loudly. After another ring, he answered the phone, not even looking at the display to see who called.

"Hello?"

"Jacob?"

"Aurora?"

"Yeah."

Jacob was surprised. He didn't know that Aurora could use a phone. Let alone, he didn't even know when she got one.

"Where are you?"

Her tone over the phone sounded worried to him. Soft and filled with a tremble.

'What's wrong?

"You haven't been home. I came by to see you. Are you okay?"

"Just driving back home now. Went out for a bit."

"I know you visited Miranda."

The comment didn't sound accusatory.

"I went looking for you originally."

He found the speed needed to travel on the highway a bit exhilarating.

"I have been busy with preparations."

"It's been a few days."

"I know, and I'm starving for you."

Those words hurt somehow. Jacob felt that it meant she only called on him for sexual things. He didn't want to be used.

"I missed you."

She was silent on the line.

"I'm sorry Jacob. You're the most important thing in the world to me and hurting you isn't what I want."

He shifted through traffic, his mood now beginning to sour.

"I want companionship," he said grumpily as he drove. "I want you, but not just the physical. If you can check in and out without considering me in that decision, what are we doing?"

Jacob understood he probably stood in the wrong unloading emotionally onto her. Aurora did have her responsibilities to the world she worked in creating. While they both worked for the goal of worshipping The Goddess, he felt abandoned. And nothing felt worse than that.

"Jacob," she spoke. "I have to be honest with you concerning that. We are getting to the point where companionship won't be difficult for you or me. I told you, what this is, what I am, is first and foremost a herald for our goddess. Trust me when I say that spending every day with you in rapturous worship is the most ideal situation for me, but then the arrival of our goddess will never be realized."

"But it's been a few days since I've seen you."

"I know, and believe me I know. You wouldn't believe the amount of stress your father

Jacob knew his father.

"What is he doing?"

"He is uh, well, handsy is one way of putting it."

Jacob wanted to believe that his father only would do something meaning that he touched unwanted places. Another possibility is that a fist touched. Unfortunately, Jacob also surmised that both could be the case. That meant that he needed to find out what actually transpired.

What did he actually do?

Devons, well, she has had better days.

"Hitting then?"

"And he does like my rear, but his lack of compatibility with us I find revolting. The only reason he is around is because of you."

Jacob almost took the last comment as her telling him to already accept it. He knew she held back on a verdict for him. Apparent to him, is that she feared upsetting him.

"Where do you want me?"

"Can you come home?"

Home.

Where was that to Jacob? He didn't know.

"I'll head over to my father's."

A pause of permeating silence filled the air. The road consistent reverberating took over as it pushed into the sphere of awareness. Jacob let the silence stand, too afraid to break it now over what Aurora would say.

"I am here already," she said, her voice flat. "Be prepared."

The call cut off.

Jacob only sighed. Something was off with Aurora. She didn't even utter a goodbye when she hung up. Maybe his refusal to act on his father upset her more than she let on. He got the hint and it soured his mood as he drove now. Even though some sex with

Aurora would be a welcome activity, he wanted to do something besides have sex with her.

"Wonder if she would like flowers," he said aloud with anger starting to grow in his chest. Thinking that it didn't matter, he drove straight to his dad's place, which did take another hour. By the time he got there, Jacob felt calmer.

Sitting in the car for a moment, he gathered his thoughts as he looked at the house.

There didn't seem to be any change in it. His observation surprised him. A few weeks ago, the place's aura felt more welcoming. Was the presence of his father tainted it? It didn't matter now as he got out of the car.

The air around him hung quietly in the air. Not even a sound of birds chirping in the air or a rustle of a nice breeze. With a sigh, he let go of his thoughts and walked into the house. There was no greeting. The quietness followed him into the house.

"Hello?"

He called out. No answer, but a scent hung in the air. A flowery pleasant scent and his cock throbbed eagerly under its smell. It confused him for a second. Why would such a thing be here?

Walking through the house, he stepped into the living room and found Aurora asleep on the couch. He stood for a moment, observing her.

Aurora didn't sleep making any noise. He could see the rhythmic rising and falling of her chest. The color of her hair was different now, colored a bright red. Her skin complexion also appeared lighter to him. Nothing new for Aurora, but she still had the petite body from the last time he saw her. Standing there, he wondered if he should wake her at all.

"Aurora," he said her name. A groan let out from her. About to call her again, she sat up abruptly.

"Jacob," she cried out in excitement and ran over to him. She embraced him in a hug and buried her head into his shoulder. A nice scent of flowers filled his nostrils and he realized that her hair felt damp against his chin. She leaned back and her pink ever-changing eyes locked with his.

He felt, at that moment, all of the foulness of his mood melt away. Without thinking, he locked lips with her and fell blissfully into a kiss.

Aurora never held back with her love. Before long, her tongue filled his mouth and her hands roamed across his back. Soon, Jacob's desire for her grew until his hands roamed over her too.

Cupping her firm buttocks in his hand, he realized how much at that moment digging fingers into her voluptuous form felt better. Then again, he would never complain about having such a wonderful woman in any form.

"I feel better," he said breaking the kiss.

"From what?"

Jacob took a breath and prepared to tell her, but then, the front door flew open startling both of them. He turned quickly as his father lumbered into the house. The patriarch stood there for a moment, but he didn't acknowledge the two of them.

"Get in here," he said. The command in his voice left no illusions about the power he exerted as Ms. Devons walked timidly in. Jacob almost exploded into anger seeing the teacher walk in.

Ms. Devons didn't look like herself.

There wasn't a smile on her face. Black-rimmed glasses sat on her face, but he could see where her eyes were puffy from crying. Everything about her was reserved and she jumped when the front door closed behind her.

"Hey dad," Jacob said, calling the man's attention to himself.

"Didn't see you there Jacob," the man responded. "Go cook something for all of us."

The command was lodged at Ms. Devons who quickly rounded the corner to disappear into the kitchen. Jacob's father smacked her on the ass as she passed, and she replied with almost sounded cute. The man then walked in before sitting on the couch. Tension in the air increased tenfold once

"What do I owe the visit?"

"Nothing, just came by to pick Aurora up."

His dad sneered before looking over to Aurora.

"She's too good for you."

"She doesn't seem to think so."

Jacob surprised himself with how quickly he spoke up. Even his father seemed to be a bit confused at his outburst. Normally, the man would have flown across the room to stamp out such a rebellious attitude. Instead, she sat back on the couch.

Remember, your girlfriend won't be here later.

"I thought I was staying the night Jacob," Aurora came up to him and latched onto his arm. She let out a whine looking up at him. It made him smile a bit.

"None of that now," his father said, ruining the moment for Jacob. He liked when Aurora played cutely. "You can stay for dinner, but I and my son will be having a conversation later that's family business."

A laugh had to be stifled with a cough from Jacob. His father didn't realize that Jacob may fear the man, but Aurora's presence alone left him feeling on a more equal footing with the abusive father.

"We can talk now if you want."

Jacob's father's head cocked in confusion.

"What, you get laid and lose some weight thinking that will make you able to stand up to me?"

His father slowly rose from the couch and squared up from across the room. Aurora's fingers dug almost painfully into his arm. Whatever transpired in the past before with Jacob's father, something would be done here. That is until a scream sounded with the crashing of dishes.

"Wait here," his father commanded at him before moving into the kitchen. Immediately, the yelling began. While that happened, Jacob began hearing Ms. Devons' cries of terror. At the first sounds of physical abuse, Jacob understood now why his father had no place in the world.

"Do what you will," He said.

'What?

I said, do what you will with him.

Jacob turned to Aurora and grabbed her into an embrace. She stiffened at the embrace. "Are you sure?" she growled.

Even if he wasn't, he knew she had begun changing even before he let her do.

"Don't use sex."

She looked up and smiled at him, showing rows of sharp teeth. Her eyes are red with excitement now.

"It's gonna be a party."

Aurora left him alone in the living room as she approached the kitchen.

"What the hell you want?"

Jacob heard his father yell at the woman as she went into the kitchen.

"What are you doing?"

There wasn't an answer with words. Instead, Jacob heard a sharp growl.

"Oh god."

The scream was cut off shortly after they began. Jacob huffed at realizing that by his own command, the last tormentor in his life now, no longer existed. Soon, after Aurora finished, he would address what to do with everything.

THE END

OTHER BOOKS BY THE AUTHOR

Cryptocurrency Millionaire Make Money
With Cryptocurrency

Secret Of Wealth Creation: Principle Lessons On
The Secrets Of Building A Long Lasting Wealth

Guide To Private Placement Project Fundingtrade
Programs: Understanding High-Level Project
Funding Trade Programs

Make Money Doing Nothing

The Blueprint To Intelligent Investors

The Blueprint To Intelligent Investors Volume 2

Financial Intelligence: Fundamentals Of Private
Placement Programs (PPP)

Private Placement Programs - The Holy Grail

Special Drawing Rights (SDR) And
The Federal Reserve

Special Drawing Rights (SDR) And
The Federal Reserve Volume 2.

Cryptocurrency: The Next Level
For Banking Reform